Backlog Studies

Charles Dudley Warner

Table of Contents

Backlog Studies

Charles Dudley Warner

FIRST STUDY

I

The fire on the hearth has almost gone out in New England; the hearth has gone out; the family has lost its center; age ceases to be respected; sex is only distinguished by a difference between millinery bills and tailors' bills; there is no more toast–and–cider; the young are not allowed to eat mince–pies at ten o'clock at night; half a cheese is no longer set to toast before the fire; you scarcely ever see in front of the coals a row of roasting apples, which a bright little girl, with many a dive and start, shielding her sunny face from the fire with one hand, turns from time to time; scarce are the gray–haired sires who strop their razors on the family Bible, and doze in the chimney–corner. A good many things have gone out with the fire on the hearth.

I do not mean to say that public and private morality have vanished with the hearth. A good degree of purity and considerable happiness are possible with grates and blowers; it is a day of trial, when we are all passing through a fiery furnace, and very likely we shall be purified as we are dried up and wasted away. Of course the family is gone, as an institution, though there still are attempts to bring up a family round a "register." But you might just as well try to bring it up by hand, as without the rallying–point of a hearthstone. Are there any homesteads nowadays? Do people hesitate to change houses any more than they do to change their clothes? People hire houses as they would a masquerade costume, liking, sometimes, to appear for a year in a little fictitious stone–front splendor above their means. Thus it happens that so many people live in houses that do not fit them. I should almost as soon think of wearing another person's clothes as his house; unless I could let it out and take it in until it fitted, and somehow expressed my own character and taste. But we have fallen into the days of conformity. It is no wonder that people constantly go into their neighbors' houses by mistake, just as, in spite of the Maine law, they wear away each other's hats from an evening party. It has almost come to this, that you might as well be anybody else as yourself.

Am I mistaken in supposing that this is owing to the discontinuance of big chimneys, with wide fireplaces in them? How can a person be attached to a house that has no center of attraction, no soul in it, in the visible form of a glowing fire, and a warm chimney, like the heart in the body? When you think of the old homestead, if you ever do, your thoughts go straight to the wide chimney and its burning logs. No wonder that you are ready to move from one fireplaceless house into another. But you have something just as good, you say. Yes, I have heard of it. This age, which imitates everything, even to the virtues of our ancestors, has invented a fireplace, with artificial, iron, or composition logs in it, hacked and painted, in which gas is burned, so that it has the appearance of a wood–fire. This seems to me blasphemy. Do you think a cat would lie down before it? Can you poke it? If you can't poke it, it is a fraud. To poke a wood–fire is more solid enjoyment than almost anything else in the world. The crowning human virtue in a man is to let his wife poke the fire. I do not know how any virtue whatever is possible over an imitation gas–log. What a sense of insincerity the family must have, if they indulge in the hypocrisy of gathering about it. With this center of untruthfulness, what must the life in the family be? Perhaps the father will be living at the rate of ten thousand a year on a salary of four thousand; perhaps the mother, more beautiful and younger than her beautified daughters, will rouge; perhaps the young ladies will make wax–work. A cynic might suggest as the motto of modern life this simple legend,—"just as good as the real." But I am not a cynic, and I hope for the rekindling of wood–fires, and a return of the beautiful home light from them. If a wood–fire is a luxury, it is cheaper than many in which we indulge without thought, and cheaper than the visits of a doctor, made necessary by the want of ventilation of the house. Not that I have anything against doctors; I only wish, after they have been to see us in a way that seems so friendly, they had nothing against us.

My fireplace, which is deep, and nearly three feet wide, has a broad hearthstone in front of it, where the live coals tumble down, and a pair of gigantic brass andirons. The brasses are burnished, and shine cheerfully in the firelight, and on either side stand tall shovel and tongs, like sentries, mounted in brass. The tongs, like the two–handed sword of

Backlog Studies

Bruce, cannot be wielded by puny people. We burn in it hickory wood, cut long. We like the smell of this aromatic forest timber, and its clear flame. The birch is also a sweet wood for the hearth, with a sort of spiritual flame and an even temper,—no snappishness. Some prefer the elm, which holds fire so well; and I have a neighbor who uses nothing but apple–tree wood,—a solid, family sort of wood, fragrant also, and full of delightful suggestions. But few people can afford to burn up their fruit trees. I should as soon think of lighting the fire with sweet–oil that comes in those graceful wicker–bound flasks from Naples, or with manuscript sermons, which, however, do not burn well, be they never so dry, not half so well as printed editorials.

Few people know how to make a wood–fire, but everybody thinks he or she does. You want, first, a large backlog, which does not rest on the andirons. This will keep your fire forward, radiate heat all day, and late in the evening fall into a ruin of glowing coals, like the last days of a good man, whose life is the richest and most beneficent at the close, when the flames of passion and the sap of youth are burned out, and there only remain the solid, bright elements of character. Then you want a forestick on the andirons; and upon these build the fire of lighter stuff. In this way you have at once a cheerful blaze, and the fire gradually eats into the solid mass, sinking down with increasing fervor; coals drop below, and delicate tongues of flame sport along the beautiful grain of the forestick. There are people who kindle a fire underneath. But these are conceited people, who are wedded to their own way. I suppose an accomplished incendiary always starts a fire in the attic, if he can. I am not an incendiary, but I hate bigotry. I don't call those incendiaries very good Christians who, when they set fire to the martyrs, touched off the fagots at the bottom, so as to make them go slow. Besides, knowledge works down easier than it does up. Education must proceed from the more enlightened down to the more ignorant strata. If you want better common schools, raise the standard of the colleges, and so on. Build your fire on top. Let your light shine. I have seen people build a fire under a balky horse; but he wouldn't go, he'd be a horse–martyr first. A fire kindled under one never did him any good. Of course you can make a fire on the hearth by kindling it underneath, but that does not make it right. I want my hearthfire to be an emblem of the best things.

II

It must be confessed that a wood–fire needs as much tending as a pair of twins. To say nothing of fiery projectiles sent into the room, even by the best wood, from the explosion

3

of gases confined in its cells, the brands are continually dropping down, and coals are being scattered over the hearth. However much a careful housewife, who thinks more of neatness than enjoyment, may dislike this, it is one of the chief delights of a wood–fire. I would as soon have an Englishman without side–whiskers as a fire without a big backlog; and I would rather have no fire than one that required no tending,—one of dead wood that could not sing again the imprisoned songs of the forest, or give out in brilliant scintillations the sunshine it absorbed in its growth. Flame is an ethereal sprite, and the spice of danger in it gives zest to the care of the hearth–fire. Nothing is so beautiful as springing, changing flame,—it was the last freak of the Gothic architecture men to represent the fronts of elaborate edifices of stone as on fire, by the kindling flamboyant devices. A fireplace is, besides, a private laboratory, where one can witness the most brilliant chemical experiments, minor conflagrations only wanting the grandeur of cities on fire. It is a vulgar notion that a fire is only for heat. A chief value of it is, however, to look at. It is a picture, framed between the jambs. You have nothing on your walls, by the best masters (the poor masters are not, however, represented), that is really so fascinating, so spiritual. Speaking like an upholsterer, it furnishes the room. And it is never twice the same. In this respect it is like the landscape–view through a window, always seen in a new light, color, or condition. The fireplace is a window into the most charming world I ever had a glimpse of.

Yet direct heat is an agreeable sensation. I am not scientific enough to despise it, and have no taste for a winter residence on Mount Washington, where the thermometer cannot be kept comfortable even by boiling. They say that they say in Boston that there is a satisfaction in being well dressed which religion cannot give. There is certainly a satisfaction in the direct radiance of a hickory fire which is not to be found in the fieriest blasts of a furnace. The hot air of a furnace is a sirocco; the heat of a wood–fire is only intense sunshine, like that bottled in Lacrimae Christi. Besides this, the eye is delighted, the sense of smell is regaled by the fragrant decomposition, and the ear is pleased with the hissing, crackling, and singing,—a liberation of so many out–door noises. Some people like the sound of bubbling in a boiling pot, or the fizzing of a frying–spider. But there is nothing gross in the animated crackling of sticks of wood blazing on the earth, not even if chestnuts are roasting in the ashes. All the senses are ministered to, and the imagination is left as free as the leaping tongues of flame.

The attention which a wood–fire demands is one of its best recommendations. We value little that which costs us no trouble to maintain. If we had to keep the sun kindled up and going by private corporate action, or act of Congress, and to be taxed for the support of customs officers of solar heat, we should prize it more than we do. Not that I should like to look upon the sun as a job, and have the proper regulation of its temperature get into politics, where we already have so much combustible stuff; but we take it quite too much as a matter of course, and, having it free, do not reckon it among the reasons for gratitude. Many people shut it out of their houses as if it were an enemy, watch its descent upon the carpet as if it were only a thief of color, and plant trees to shut it away from the mouldering house. All the animals know better than this, as well as the more simple races of men; the old women of the southern Italian coasts sit all day in the sun and ply the distaff, as grateful as the sociable hens on the south side of a New England barn; the slow tortoise likes to take the sun upon his sloping back, soaking in color that shall make him immortal when the imperishable part of him is cut up into shell ornaments. The capacity of a cat to absorb sunshine is only equaled by that of an Arab or an Ethiopian. They are not afraid of injuring their complexions.

White must be the color of civilization; it has so many natural disadvantages. But this is politics. I was about to say that, however it may be with sunshine, one is always grateful for his wood–fire, because he does not maintain it without some cost.

Yet I cannot but confess to a difference between sunlight and the light of a wood–fire. The sunshine is entirely untamed. Where it rages most freely it tends to evoke the brilliancy rather than the harmonious satisfactions of nature. The monstrous growths and the flaming colors of the tropics contrast with our more subdued loveliness of foliage and bloom. The birds of the middle region dazzle with their contrasts of plumage, and their voices are for screaming rather than singing. I presume the new experiments in sound would project a macaw's voice in very tangled and inharmonious lines of light. I suspect that the fiercest sunlight puts people, as well as animals and vegetables, on extremes in all ways. A wood–fire on the hearth is a kindler of the domestic virtues. It brings in cheerfulness, and a family center, and, besides, it is artistic. I should like to know if an artist could ever represent on canvas a happy family gathered round a hole in the floor called a register. Given a fireplace, and a tolerable artist could almost create a pleasant family round it. But what could he conjure out of a register? If there was any virtue among our ancestors,—and they labored under a great many disadvantages, and had few of the aids which we have to excellence of life,—I am convinced they drew it mostly from the fireside. If it was difficult to read the eleven commandments by the light of a pine–knot, it was not difficult to get the sweet spirit of them from the countenance of the serene mother knitting in the chimney—corner.

III

When the fire is made, you want to sit in front of it and grow genial in its effulgence. I have never been upon a throne,—except in moments of a traveler's curiosity, about as long as a South American dictator remains on one,—but I have no idea that it compares, for pleasantness, with a seat before a wood—fire. A whole leisure day before you, a good novel in hand, and the backlog only just beginning to kindle, with uncounted hours of comfort in it, has life anything more delicious? For "novel" you can substitute "Calvin's Institutes," if you wish to be virtuous as well as happy. Even Calvin would melt before a wood—fire. A great snowstorm, visible on three sides of your wide—windowed room, loading the evergreens, blown in fine powder from the great chestnut—tops, piled up in ever accumulating masses, covering the paths, the shrubbery, the hedges, drifting and clinging in fantastic deposits, deepening your sense of security, and taking away the sin of idleness by making it a necessity, this is an excellent ground to your day by the fire.

To deliberately sit down in the morning to read a novel, to enjoy yourself, is this not, in New England (I am told they don't read much in other parts of the country), the sin of sins? Have you any right to read, especially novels, until you have exhausted the best part of the day in some employment that is called practical? Have you any right to enjoy yourself at all until the fag—end of the day, when you are tired and incapable of enjoying yourself? I am aware that this is the practice, if not the theory, of our society,—to postpone the delights of social intercourse until after dark, and rather late at night, when body and mind are both weary with the exertions of business, and when we can give to what is the most delightful and profitable thing in life, social and intellectual society, only the weariness of dull brains and over—tired muscles. No wonder we take our amusements sadly, and that so many people find dinners heavy and parties stupid. Our economy leaves no place for amusements; we merely add them to the burden of a life already full. The world is still a little off the track as to what is really useful.

I confess that the morning is a very good time to read a novel, or anything else which is good and requires a fresh mind; and I take it that nothing is worth reading that does not require an alert mind. I suppose it is necessary that business should be transacted; though the amount of business that does not contribute to anybody's comfort or improvement suggests the query whether it is not overdone. I know that unremitting attention to business is the price of success, but I don't know what success is. There is a man, whom we all know, who built a house that cost a quarter of a million of dollars, and furnished it for another like sum, who does not know anything more about architecture, or painting, or books, or history, than he cares for the rights of those who have not so much money as he has. I heard him once, in a foreign gallery, say to his wife, as they stood in front of a famous picture by Rubens: "That is the Rape of the Sardines!" What a cheerful world it would be if everybody was as successful as that man! While I am reading my book by the fire, and taking an active part in important transactions that may be a good deal better than real, let me be thankful that a great many men are profitably employed in offices and bureaus and country stores in keeping up the gossip and endless exchange of opinions among mankind, so much of which is made to appear to the women at home as "business." I find that there is a sort of busy idleness among men in this world that is not held in disrepute. When the time comes that I have to prove my right to vote, with women, I trust that it will be remembered in my favor that I made this admission. If it is true, as a witty conservative once said to me, that we never shall have peace in this country until we elect a colored woman president, I desire to be rectus in curia early.

IV

The fireplace, as we said, is a window through which we look out upon other scenes. We like to read of the small, bare room, with cobwebbed ceiling and narrow window, in which the poor child of genius sits with his magical pen, the master of a realm of beauty and enchantment. I think the open fire does not kindle the imagination so much as it awakens the memory; one sees the past in its crumbling embers and ashy grayness, rather than the future. People become reminiscent and even sentimental in front of it. They used to become something else in those good old days when it was thought best to heat the poker red hot before plunging it into the mugs of flip. This heating of the poker has been disapproved of late years, but I do not know on what grounds; if one is to drink bitters and gins and the like, such as I understand as good people as clergymen and women take in private, and by advice, I do not know why one should not make them palatable and heat them with his own poker. Cold whiskey out of a bottle, taken as a prescription six times a day on the sly, is n't my idea of virtue any more than the social ancestral glass, sizzling wickedly with the hot iron. Names are so confusing in this world; but things are apt to remain pretty much the same, whatever we call them.

Backlog Studies

Perhaps as you look into the fireplace it widens and grows deep and cavernous. The back and the jambs are built up of great stones, not always smoothly laid, with jutting ledges upon which ashes are apt to lie. The hearthstone is an enormous block of trap rock, with a surface not perfectly even, but a capital place to crack butternuts on. Over the fire swings an iron crane, with a row of pot–hooks of all lengths hanging from it. It swings out when the housewife wants to hang on the tea–kettle, and it is strong enough to support a row of pots, or a mammoth caldron kettle on occasion. What a jolly sight is this fireplace when the pots and kettles in a row are all boiling and bubbling over the flame, and a roasting spit is turning in front! It makes a person as hungry as one of Scott's novels. But the brilliant sight is in the frosty morning, about daylight, when the fire is made. The coals are raked open, the split sticks are piled up in openwork criss–crossing, as high as the crane; and when the flame catches hold and roars up through the interstices, it is like an out–of–door bonfire. Wood enough is consumed in that morning sacrifice to cook the food of a Parisian family for a year. How it roars up the wide chimney, sending into the air the signal smoke and sparks which announce to the farming neighbors another day cheerfully begun! The sleepiest boy in the world would get up in his red flannel nightgown to see such a fire lighted, even if he dropped to sleep again in his chair before the ruddy blaze. Then it is that the house, which has shrunk and creaked all night in the pinching cold of winter, begins to glow again and come to life. The thick frost melts little by little on the small window–panes, and it is seen that the gray dawn is breaking over the leagues of pallid snow. It is time to blow out the candle, which has lost all its cheerfulness in the light of day. The morning romance is over; the family is astir; and member after member appears with the morning yawn, to stand before the crackling, fierce conflagration. The daily round begins. The most hateful employment ever invented for mortal man presents itself: the "chores" are to be done. The boy who expects every morning to open into a new world finds that to–day is like yesterday, but he believes to–morrow will be different. And yet enough for him, for the day, is the wading in the snowdrifts, or the sliding on the diamond–sparkling crust. Happy, too, is he, when the storm rages, and the snow is piled high against the windows, if he can sit in the warm chimney– corner and read about Burgoyne, and General Fraser, and Miss McCrea, midwinter marches through the wilderness, surprises of wigwams, and the stirring ballad, say, of the Battle of the Kegs:—

"Come, gallants, attend and list a friend Thrill forth harmonious ditty; While I shall tell what late befell At Philadelphia city."

I should like to know what heroism a boy in an old New England farmhouse—rough-nursed by nature, and fed on the traditions of the old wars did not aspire to. "John," says the mother, "You'll burn your head to a crisp in that heat." But John does not hear; he is storming the Plains of Abraham just now. "Johnny, dear, bring in a stick of wood." How can Johnny bring in wood when he is in that defile with Braddock, and the Indians are popping at him from behind every tree? There is something about a boy that I like, after all.

The fire rests upon the broad hearth; the hearth rests upon a great substruction of stone, and the substruction rests upon the cellar. What supports the cellar I never knew, but the cellar supports the family. The cellar is the foundation of domestic comfort. Into its dark, cavernous recesses the child's imagination fearfully goes. Bogies guard the bins of choicest apples. I know not what comical sprites sit astride the cider-barrels ranged along the walls. The feeble flicker of the tallow-candle does not at all dispel, but creates, illusions, and magnifies all the rich possibilities of this underground treasure-house. When the cellar-door is opened, and the boy begins to descend into the thick darkness, it is always with a heart-beat as of one started upon some adventure. Who can forget the smell that comes through the opened door;—a mingling of fresh earth, fruit exhaling delicious aroma, kitchen vegetables, the mouldy odor of barrels, a sort of ancestral air,—as if a door had been opened into an old romance. Do you like it? Not much. But then I would not exchange the remembrance of it for a good many odors and perfumes that I do like.

It is time to punch the backlog and put on a new forestick.

SECOND STUDY

I

The log was white birch. The beautiful satin bark at once kindled into a soft, pure, but brilliant flame, something like that of naphtha. There is no other wood flame so rich, and it leaps up in a joyous, spiritual way, as if glad to burn for the sake of burning. Burning like a clear oil, it has none of the heaviness and fatness of the pine and the balsam. Woodsmen are at a loss to account for its intense and yet chaste flame, since the bark has no oily appearance. The heat from it is fierce, and the light dazzling. It flares up eagerly like young love, and then dies away; the wood does not keep up the promise of the bark. The woodsmen, it is proper to say, have not considered it in its relation to young love. In the remote settlements the pine–knot is still the torch of courtship; it endures to sit up by. The birch–bark has alliances with the world of sentiment and of letters. The most poetical reputation of the North American Indian floats in a canoe made of it; his picture–writing was inscribed on it. It is the paper that nature furnishes for lovers in the wilderness, who are enabled to convey a delicate sentiment by its use, which is expressed neither in their ideas nor chirography. It is inadequate for legal parchment, but does very well for deeds of love, which are not meant usually to give a perfect title. With care, it may be split into sheets as thin as the Chinese paper. It is so beautiful to handle that it is a pity civilization cannot make more use of it. But fancy articles manufactured from it are very much like all ornamental work made of nature's perishable seeds, leaves, cones, and dry twigs,—exquisite while the pretty fingers are fashioning it, but soon growing shabby and cheap to the eye. And yet there is a pathos in "dried things," whether they are displayed as ornaments in some secluded home, or hidden religiously in bureau drawers where profane eyes cannot see how white ties are growing yellow and ink is fading from treasured letters, amid a faint and discouraging perfume of ancient rose–leaves.

The birch log holds out very well while it is green, but has not substance enough for a backlog when dry. Seasoning green timber or men is always an experiment. A man may do very well in a simple, let us say, country or backwoods line of life, who would come to nothing in a more complicated civilization. City life is a severe trial. One man is struck with a dry–rot; another develops season–cracks; another shrinks and swells with every change of circumstance. Prosperity is said to be more trying than adversity, a theory which most people are willing to accept without trial; but few men stand the drying out of the natural sap of their greenness in the artificial heat of city life. This, be it noticed, is nothing against the drying and seasoning process; character must be put into the crucible some time, and why not in this world? A man who cannot stand seasoning will not have a high market value in any part of the universe. It is creditable to the race, that so many men and women bravely jump into the furnace of prosperity and expose themselves to the drying influences of city life.

The first fire that is lighted on the hearth in the autumn seems to bring out the cold weather. Deceived by the placid appearance of the dying year, the softness of the sky, and the warm color of the foliage, we have been shivering about for days without exactly comprehending what was the matter. The open fire at once sets up a standard of comparison. We find that the advance guards of winter are besieging the house. The cold rushes in at every crack of door and window, apparently signaled by the flame to invade the house and fill it with chilly drafts and sarcasms on what we call the temperate zone. It needs a roaring fire to beat back the enemy; a feeble one is only an invitation to the most insulting demonstrations. Our pious New England ancestors were philosophers in their way. It was not simply owing to grace that they sat for hours in their barnlike meeting−houses during the winter Sundays, the thermometer many degrees below freezing, with no fire, except the zeal in their own hearts,—a congregation of red noses and bright eyes. It was no wonder that the minister in the pulpit warmed up to his subject, cried aloud, used hot words, spoke a good deal of the hot place and the Person whose presence was a burning shame, hammered the desk as if he expected to drive his text through a two−inch plank, and heated himself by all allowable ecclesiastical gymnastics. A few of their followers in our day seem to forget that our modern churches are heated by furnaces and supplied with gas. In the old days it would have been thought unphilosophic as well as effeminate to warm the meeting−houses artificially. In one house I knew, at least, when it was proposed to introduce a stove to take a little of the chill from the Sunday services, the deacons protested against the innovation. They said that the stove might benefit those who sat close to it, but it would drive all the cold air to the other parts of the church, and freeze the people to death; it was cold enough now around the edges. Blessed days of ignorance and upright living! Sturdy men who served God by resolutely sitting out the icy hours of service, amid the rattling of windows and the carousal of winter in the high, windswept galleries! Patient women, waiting in the chilly house for consumption to pick out his victims, and replace the color of youth and the flush of devotion with the hectic of disease! At least, you did not doze and droop in our over−heated edifices, and die of vitiated air and disregard of the simplest conditions of organized life. It is fortunate that each generation does not comprehend its own ignorance. We are thus enabled to call our ancestors barbarous. It is something also that each age has its choice of the death it will die. Our generation is most ingenious. From our public assembly−rooms and houses we have almost succeeded in excluding pure air. It took the race ages to build dwellings that would keep out rain; it has taken longer to build houses air−tight, but we are on the eve of success. We are only foiled by the ill−fitting, insincere work of the builders, who build for a day, and charge for all time.

II

Backlog Studies

When the fire on the hearth has blazed up and then settled into steady radiance, talk begins. There is no place like the chimney– corner for confidences; for picking up the clews of an old friendship; for taking note where one's self has drifted, by comparing ideas and prejudices with the intimate friend of years ago, whose course in life has lain apart from yours. No stranger puzzles you so much as the once close friend, with whose thinking and associates you have for years been unfamiliar. Life has come to mean this and that to you; you have fallen into certain habits of thought; for you the world has progressed in this or that direction; of certain results you feel very sure; you have fallen into harmony with your surroundings; you meet day after day people interested in the things that interest you; you are not in the least opinionated, it is simply your good fortune to look upon the affairs of the world from the right point of view. When you last saw your friend,—less than a year after you left college,—he was the most sensible and agreeable of men; he had no heterodox notions; he agreed with you; you could even tell what sort of a wife he would select, and if you could do that, you held the key to his life.

Well, Herbert came to visit me the other day from the antipodes. And here he sits by the fireplace. I cannot think of any one I would rather see there, except perhaps Thackery; or, for entertainment, Boswell; or old, Pepys; or one of the people who was left out of the Ark. They were talking one foggy London night at Hazlitt's about whom they would most like to have seen, when Charles Lamb startled the company by declaring that he would rather have seen Judas Iscariot than any other person who had lived on the earth. For myself, I would rather have seen Lamb himself once, than to have lived with Judas. Herbert, to my great delight, has not changed; I should know him anywhere,—the same serious, contemplative face, with lurking humor at the corners of the mouth,—the same cheery laugh and clear, distinct enunciation as of old. There is nothing so winning as a good voice. To see Herbert again, unchanged in all outward essentials, is not only gratifying, but valuable as a testimony to nature's success in holding on to a personal identity, through the entire change of matter that has been constantly taking place for so many years. I know very well there is here no part of the Herbert whose hand I had shaken at the Commencement parting; but it is an astonishing reproduction of him,—a material likeness; and now for the spiritual.

Such a wide chance for divergence in the spiritual. It has been such a busy world for twenty years. So many things have been torn up by the roots again that were settled when we left college. There were to be no more wars; democracy was democracy, and progress, the differentiation of the individual, was a mere question of clothes; if you want

12

to be different, go to your tailor; nobody had demonstrated that there is a man—soul and a woman—soul, and that each is in reality only a half—soul,—putting the race, so to speak, upon the half—shell. The social oyster being opened, there appears to be two shells and only one oyster; who shall have it? So many new canons of taste, of criticism, of morality have been set up; there has been such a resurrection of historical reputations for new judgment, and there have been so many discoveries, geographical, archaeological, geological, biological, that the earth is not at all what it was supposed to be; and our philosophers are much more anxious to ascertain where we came from than whither we are going. In this whirl and turmoil of new ideas, nature, which has only the single end of maintaining the physical identity in the body, works on undisturbed, replacing particle for particle, and preserving the likeness more skillfully than a mosaic artist in the Vatican; she has not even her materials sorted and labeled, as the Roman artist has his thousands of bits of color; and man is all the while doing his best to confuse the process, by changing his climate, his diet, all his surroundings, without the least care to remain himself. But the mind?

It is more difficult to get acquainted with Herbert than with an entire stranger, for I have my prepossessions about him, and do not find him in so many places where I expect to find him. He is full of criticism of the authors I admire; he thinks stupid or improper the books I most read; he is skeptical about the "movements" I am interested in; he has formed very different opinions from mine concerning a hundred men and women of the present day; we used to eat from one dish; we could n't now find anything in common in a dozen; his prejudices (as we call our opinions) are most extraordinary, and not half so reasonable as my prejudices; there are a great many persons and things that I am accustomed to denounce, uncontradicted by anybody, which he defends; his public opinion is not at all my public opinion. I am sorry for him. He appears to have fallen into influences and among a set of people foreign to me. I find that his church has a different steeple on it from my church (which, to say the truth, hasn't any). It is a pity that such a dear friend and a man of so much promise should have drifted off into such general contrariness. I see Herbert sitting here by the fire, with the old look in his face coming out more and more, but I do not recognize any features of his mind,—except perhaps his contrariness; yes, he was always a little contrary, I think. And finally he surprises me with, "Well, my friend, you seem to have drifted away from your old notions and opinions. We used to agree when we were together, but I sometimes wondered where you would land; for, pardon me, you showed signs of looking at things a little contrary."

Backlog Studies

I am silent for a good while. I am trying to think who I am. There was a person whom I thought I knew, very fond of Herbert, and agreeing with him in most things. Where has he gone? and, if he is here, where is the Herbert that I knew?

If his intellectual and moral sympathies have all changed, I wonder if his physical tastes remain, like his appearance, the same. There has come over this country within the last generation, as everybody knows, a great wave of condemnation of pie. It has taken the character of a "movement!" though we have had no conventions about it, nor is any one, of any of the several sexes among us, running for president against it. It is safe almost anywhere to denounce pie, yet nearly everybody eats it on occasion. A great many people think it savors of a life abroad to speak with horror of pie, although they were very likely the foremost of the Americans in Paris who used to speak with more enthusiasm of the American pie at Madame Busque's than of the Venus of Milo. To talk against pie and still eat it is snobbish, of course; but snobbery, being an aspiring failing, is sometimes the prophecy of better things. To affect dislike of pie is something. We have no statistics on the subject, and cannot tell whether it is gaining or losing in the country at large. Its disappearance in select circles is no test. The amount of writing against it is no more test of its desuetude, than the number of religious tracts distributed in a given district is a criterion of its piety. We are apt to assume that certain regions are substantially free of it. Herbert and I, traveling north one summer, fancied that we could draw in New England a sort of diet line, like the sweeping curves on the isothermal charts, which should show at least the leading pie sections. Journeying towards the White Mountains, we concluded that a line passing through Bellows Falls, and bending a little south on either side, would mark northward the region of perpetual pie. In this region pie is to be found at all hours and seasons, and at every meal. I am not sure, however, that pie is not a matter of altitude rather than latitude, as I find that all the hill and country towns of New England are full of those excellent women, the very salt of the housekeeping earth, who would feel ready to sink in mortification through their scoured kitchen floors, if visitors should catch them without a pie in the house. The absence of pie would be more noticed than a scarcity of Bible even. Without it the housekeepers are as distracted as the boarding–house keeper, who declared that if it were not for canned tomato, she should have nothing to fly to. Well, in all this great agitation I find Herbert unmoved, a conservative, even to the under–crust. I dare not ask him if he eats pie at breakfast. There are some tests that the dearest friendship may not apply.

"Will you smoke?" I ask.

Backlog Studies

"No, I have reformed."

"Yes, of course."

"The fact is, that when we consider the correlation of forces, the apparent sympathy of spirit manifestations with electric conditions, the almost revealed mysteries of what may be called the odic force, and the relation of all these phenomena to the nervous system in man, it is not safe to do anything to the nervous system that will—"

"Hang the nervous system! Herbert, we can agree in one thing: old memories, reveries, friendships, center about that:—is n't an open wood–fire good?"

"Yes," says Herbert, combatively, "if you don't sit before it too long."

III

The best talk is that which escapes up the open chimney and cannot be repeated. The finest woods make the best fire and pass away with the least residuum. I hope the next generation will not accept the reports of "interviews" as specimens of the conversations of these years of grace.

But do we talk as well as our fathers and mothers did? We hear wonderful stories of the bright generation that sat about the wide fireplaces of New England. Good talk has so much short–hand that it cannot be reported,—the inflection, the change of voice, the shrug, cannot be caught on paper. The best of it is when the subject unexpectedly goes cross–lots, by a flash of short–cut, to a conclusion so suddenly revealed that it has the effect of wit. It needs the highest culture and the finest breeding to prevent the conversation from running into mere persiflage on the one hand—its common fate—or monologue on the other. Our conversation is largely chaff. I am not sure but the former generation preached a good deal, but it had great practice in fireside talk, and must have talked well. There were narrators in those days who could charm a circle all the evening long with stories. When each day brought comparatively little new to read, there was leisure for talk, and the rare book and the in–frequent magazine were thoroughly discussed. Families now are swamped by the printed matter that comes daily upon the center–table. There must be a division of labor, one reading this, and another that, to make any impression on it. The telegraph brings the only common food, and works this daily miracle, that every mind in Christendom is excited by one topic simultaneously with every other mind; it enables a concurrent mental action, a burst of sympathy, or a universal prayer to be made, which must be, if we have any faith in the immaterial left, one of the chief forces in modern life. It is fit that an agent so subtle as electricity should be the minister of it.

When there is so much to read, there is little time for conversation; nor is there leisure for another pastime of the ancient firesides, called reading aloud. The listeners, who heard while they looked into the wide chimney–place, saw there pass in stately procession the events and the grand persons of history, were kindled with the delights of travel, touched by the romance of true love, or made restless by tales of adventure;—the hearth became a sort of magic stone that could transport those who sat by it to the most distant places and times, as soon as the book was opened and the reader began, of a winter's night. Perhaps the Puritan reader read through his nose, and all the little Puritans made the most dreadful nasal inquiries as the entertainment went on. The prominent nose of the intellectual New–Englander is evidence of the constant linguistic exercise of the organ for generations. It grew by talking through. But I have no doubt that practice made good readers in those days. Good reading aloud is almost a lost accomplishment now. It is little thought of in the schools. It is disused at home. It is rare to find any one who can read, even from the newspaper, well. Reading is so universal, even with the uncultivated, that it is common to hear people mispronounce words that you did not suppose they had ever seen. In reading to themselves they glide over these words, in reading aloud they stumble over them. Besides, our every–day books and newspapers are so larded with French that the ordinary reader is obliged marcher a pas de loup,—for instance.

The newspaper is probably responsible for making current many words with which the general reader is familiar, but which he rises to in the flow of conversation, and strikes at with a splash and an unsuccessful attempt at appropriation; the word, which he perfectly knows, hooks him in the gills, and he cannot master it. The newspaper is thus widening the language in use, and vastly increasing the number of words which enter into common talk. The Americans of the lowest intellectual class probably use more words to express their ideas than the similar class of any other people; but this prodigality is partially balanced by the parsimony of words in some higher regions, in which a few phrases of current slang are made to do the whole duty of exchange of ideas; if that can be called exchange of ideas when one intellect flashes forth to another the remark, concerning some report, that "you know how it is yourself," and is met by the response of "that's what's the matter," and rejoins with the perfectly conclusive "that's so." It requires a high degree of culture to use slang with elegance and effect; and we are yet very far from the Greek attainment.

IV

The fireplace wants to be all aglow, the wind rising, the night heavy and black above, but light with sifting snow on the earth, a background of inclemency for the illumined room with its pictured walls, tables heaped with books, capacious easy–chairs and their occupants,—it needs, I say, to glow and throw its rays far through the crystal of the broad windows, in order that we may rightly appreciate the relation of the wide–jambed chimney to domestic architecture in our climate. We fell to talking about it; and, as is usual when the conversation is professedly on one subject, we wandered all around it. The young lady staying with us was roasting chestnuts in the ashes, and the frequent explosions required considerable attention. The mistress, too, sat somewhat alert, ready to rise at any instant and minister to the fancied want of this or that guest, forgetting the reposeful truth that people about a fireside will not have any wants if they are not suggested. The worst of them, if they desire anything, only want something hot, and that later in the evening. And it is an open question whether you ought to associate with people who want that.

I was saying that nothing had been so slow in its progress in the world as domestic architecture. Temples, palaces, bridges, aqueducts, cathedrals, towers of marvelous delicacy and strength, grew to perfection while the common people lived in hovels, and the richest lodged in the most gloomy and contracted quarters. The dwelling–house is a modern institution. It is a curious fact that it has only improved with the social elevation of women. Men were never more brilliant in arms and letters than in the age of Elizabeth, and yet they had no homes. They made themselves thick–walled castles, with slits in the masonry for windows, for defense, and magnificent banquet–halls for pleasure; the stone rooms into which they crawled for the night were often little better than dog–kennels. The Pompeians had no comfortable night–quarters. The most singular thing to me, however, is that, especially interested as woman is in the house, she has never done anything for architecture. And yet woman is reputed to be an ingenious creature.

HERBERT. I doubt if woman has real ingenuity; she has great adaptability. I don't say that she will do the same thing twice alike, like a Chinaman, but she is most cunning in suiting herself to circumstances.

THE FIRE–TENDER. Oh, if you speak of constructive, creative ingenuity, perhaps not; but in the higher ranges of achievement—that of accomplishing any purpose dear to her heart, for instance—her ingenuity is simply incomprehensible to me.

HERBERT. Yes, if you mean doing things by indirection.

THE MISTRESS. When you men assume all the direction, what else is left to us?

THE FIRE–TENDER. Did you ever see a woman refurnish a house?

THE YOUNG LADY STAYING WITH US. I never saw a man do it, unless he was burned out of his rookery.

HERBERT. There is no comfort in new things.

THE FIRE–TENDER (not noticing the interruption). Having set her mind on a total revolution of the house, she buys one new thing, not too obtrusive, nor much out of harmony with the old. The husband scarcely notices it, least of all does he suspect the revolution, which she already has accomplished. Next, some article that does look a little shabby beside the new piece of furniture is sent to the garret, and its place is supplied by something that will match in color and effect. Even the man can see that it ought to match, and so the process goes on, it may be for years, it may be forever, until nothing of the old is left, and the house is transformed as it was predetermined in the woman's mind. I doubt if the man ever understands how or when it was done; his wife certainly never says anything about the refurnishing, but quietly goes on to new conquests.

THE MISTRESS. And is n't it better to buy little by little, enjoying every new object as you get it, and assimilating each article to your household life, and making the home a harmonious expression of your own taste, rather than to order things in sets, and turn your house, for the time being, into a furniture ware–room?

THE FIRE–TENDER. Oh, I only spoke of the ingenuity of it.

THE YOUNG LADY. For my part, I never can get acquainted with more than one piece of furniture at a time.

HERBERT. I suppose women are our superiors in artistic taste, and I fancy that I can tell whether a house is furnished by a woman or a man; of course, I mean the few houses that appear to be the result of individual taste and refinement,—most of them look as if they had been furnished on contract by the upholsterer.

THE MISTRESS. Woman's province in this world is putting things to rights.

HERBERT. With a vengeance, sometimes. In the study, for example. My chief objection to woman is that she has no respect for the newspaper, or the printed page, as such. She is Siva, the destroyer. I have noticed that a great part of a married man's time at home is spent in trying to find the things he has put on his study–table.

THE YOUNG LADY. Herbert speaks with the bitterness of a bachelor shut out of paradise. It is my experience that if women did not destroy the rubbish that men bring into the house, it would become uninhabitable, and need to be burned down every five years.

THE FIRE–TENDER. I confess women do a great deal for the appearance of things. When the mistress is absent, this room, although everything is here as it was before, does not look at all like the same place; it is stiff, and seems to lack a soul. When she returns, I can see that her eye, even while greeting me, takes in the situation at a glance. While she is talking of the journey, and before she has removed her traveling–hat, she turns this chair and moves that, sets one piece of furniture at a different angle, rapidly, and apparently unconsciously, shifts a dozen little knick–knacks and bits of color, and the room is transformed. I couldn't do it in a week.

THE MISTRESS. That is the first time I ever knew a man admit he couldn't do anything if he had time.

HERBERT. Yet with all their peculiar instinct for making a home, women make themselves very little felt in our domestic architecture.

THE MISTRESS. Men build most of the houses in what might be called the ready–made–clothing style, and we have to do the best we can with them; and hard enough it is to make cheerful homes in most of them. You will see something different when the woman is constantly consulted in the plan of the house.

HERBERT. We might see more difference if women would give any attention to architecture. Why are there no women architects?

THE FIRE–TENDER. Want of the ballot, doubtless. It seems to me that here is a splendid opportunity for woman to come to the front.

THE YOUNG LADY. They have no desire to come to the front; they would rather manage things where they are.

THE FIRE–TENDER. If they would master the noble art, and put their brooding taste upon it, we might very likely compass something in our domestic architecture that we have not yet attained. The outside of our houses needs attention as well as the inside. Most of them are as ugly as money can build.

THE YOUNG LADY. What vexes me most is, that women, married women, have so easily consented to give up open fires in their houses.

HERBERT. They dislike the dust and the bother. I think that women rather like the confined furnace heat.

THE FIRE–TENDER. Nonsense; it is their angelic virtue of submission. We wouldn't be hired to stay all–day in the houses we build.

THE YOUNG LADY. That has a very chivalrous sound, but I know there will be no reformation until women rebel and demand everywhere the open fire.

HERBERT. They are just now rebelling about something else; it seems to me yours is a sort of counter–movement, a fire in the rear.

THE MISTRESS. I'll join that movement. The time has come when woman must strike for her altars and her fires.

HERBERT. Hear, hear!

THE MISTRESS. Thank you, Herbert. I applauded you once, when you declaimed that years ago in the old Academy. I remember how eloquently you did it.

HERBERT. Yes, I was once a spouting idiot.

Just then the door–bell rang, and company came in. And the company brought in a new atmosphere, as company always does, something of the disturbance of out–doors, and a good deal of its healthy cheer. The direct news that the thermometer was approaching zero, with a hopeful prospect of going below it, increased to liveliness our satisfaction in the fire. When the cider was heated in the brown stone pitcher, there was difference of opinion whether there should be toast in it; some were for toast, because that was the old–fashioned way, and others were against it, "because it does not taste good" in cider. Herbert said there, was very little respect left for our forefathers.

More wood was put on, and the flame danced in a hundred fantastic shapes. The snow had ceased to fall, and the moonlight lay in silvery patches among the trees in the ravine. The conversation became worldly.

THIRD STUDY

I

Herbert said, as we sat by the fire one night, that he wished he had turned his attention to writing poetry like Tennyson's.

The remark was not whimsical, but satirical. Tennyson is a man of talent, who happened to strike a lucky vein, which he has worked with cleverness. The adventurer with a pickaxe in Washoe may happen upon like good fortune. The world is full of poetry as the earth is of "pay–dirt;" one only needs to know how to "strike" it. An able man can make himself almost anything that he will. It is melancholy to think how many epic poets have been lost in the tea–trade, how many dramatists (though the age of the drama has passed) have wasted their genius in great mercantile and mechanical enterprises. I know a man who might have been the poet, the essayist, perhaps the critic, of this country, who chose to become a country judge, to sit day after day upon a bench in an obscure corner of the world, listening to wrangling lawyers and prevaricating witnesses, preferring to judge his fellow—men rather than enlighten them.

It is fortunate for the vanity of the living and the reputation of the dead, that men get almost as much credit for what they do not as for what they do. It was the opinion of many that Burns might have excelled as a statesman, or have been a great captain in war; and Mr. Carlyle says that if he had been sent to a university, and become a trained intellectual workman, it lay in him to have changed the whole course of British literature! A large undertaking, as so vigorous and dazzling a writer as Mr. Carlyle must know by this time, since British literature has swept by him in a resistless and widening flood, mainly uncontaminated, and leaving his grotesque contrivances wrecked on the shore with other curiosities of letters, and yet among the richest of all the treasures lying there.

It is a temptation to a temperate man to become a sot, to hear what talent, what versatility, what genius, is almost always attributed to a moderately bright man who is habitually drunk. Such a mechanic, such a mathematician, such a poet he would be, if he were only sober; and then he is sure to be the most generous, magnanimous, friendly soul, conscientiously honorable, if he were not so conscientiously drunk. I suppose it is now notorious that the most brilliant and promising men have been lost to the world in this way. It is sometimes almost painful to think what a surplus of talent and genius there would be in the world if the habit of intoxication should suddenly cease; and what a slim chance there would be for the plodding people who have always had tolerably good habits. The fear is only mitigated by the observation that the reputation of a person for great talent sometimes ceases with his reformation.

It is believed by some that the maidens who would make the best wives never marry, but remain free to bless the world with their impartial sweetness, and make it generally habitable. This is one of the mysteries of Providence and New England life. It seems a pity, at first sight, that all those who become poor wives have the matrimonial chance, and that they are deprived of the reputation of those who would be good wives were they not set apart for the high and perpetual office of priestesses of society. There is no beauty like that which was spoiled by an accident, no accomplishments—and graces are so to be envied as those that circumstances rudely hindered the development of. All of which shows what a charitable and good—tempered world it is, notwithstanding its reputation for cynicism and detraction.

Backlog Studies

Nothing is more beautiful than the belief of the faithful wife that her husband has all the talents, and could , if he would, be distinguished in any walk in life; and nothing will be more beautiful—unless this is a very dry time for signs—than the husband's belief that his wife is capable of taking charge of any of the affairs of this confused planet. There is no woman but thinks that her husband, the green—grocer, could write poetry if he had given his mind to it, or else she thinks small beer of poetry in comparison with an occupation or accomplishment purely vegetable. It is touching to see the look of pride with which the wife turns to her husband from any more brilliant personal presence or display of wit than his, in the perfect confidence that if the world knew what she knows, there would be one more popular idol. How she magnifies his small wit, and dotes upon the self—satisfied look in his face as if it were a sign of wisdom! What a councilor that man would make! What a warrior he would be! There are a great many corporals in their retired homes who did more for the safety and success of our armies in critical moments, in the late war, than any of the "high— cock—a—lorum" commanders. Mrs. Corporal does not envy the reputation of General Sheridan; she knows very well who really won Five Forks, for she has heard the story a hundred times, and will hear it a hundred times more with apparently unabated interest. What a general her husband would have made; and how his talking talent would shine in Congress!

HERBERT. Nonsense. There isn't a wife in the world who has not taken the exact measure of her husband, weighed him and settled him in her own mind, and knows him as well as if she had ordered him after designs and specifications of her own. That knowledge, however, she ordinarily keeps to herself, and she enters into a league with her husband, which he was never admitted to the secret of, to impose upon the world. In nine out of ten cases he more than half believes that he is what his wife tells him he is. At any rate, she manages him as easily as the keeper does the elephant, with only a bamboo wand and a sharp spike in the end. Usually she flatters him, but she has the means of pricking clear through his hide on occasion. It is the great secret of her power to have him think that she thoroughly believes in him.

THE YOUNG LADY STAYING WITH Us. And you call this hypocrisy? I have heard authors, who thought themselves sly observers of women, call it so.

HERBERT. Nothing of the sort. It is the basis on which society rests, the conventional agreement. If society is about to be overturned, it is on this point. Women are beginning to tell men what they really think of them; and to insist that the same relations of downright sincerity and independence that exist between men shall exist between women and men. Absolute truth between souls, without regard to sex, has always been the ideal life of the poets.

THE MISTRESS. Yes; but there was never a poet yet who would bear to have his wife say exactly what she thought of his poetry, any more than be would keep his temper if his wife beat him at chess; and there is nothing that disgusts a man like getting beaten at chess by a woman.

HERBERT. Well, women know how to win by losing. I think that the reason why most women do not want to take the ballot and stand out in the open for a free trial of power, is that they are reluctant to change the certain domination of centuries, with weapons they are perfectly competent to handle, for an experiment. I think we should be better off if women were more transparent, and men were not so systematically puffed up by the subtle flattery which is used to control them.

MANDEVILLE. Deliver me from transparency. When a woman takes that guise, and begins to convince me that I can see through her like a ray of light, I must run or be lost. Transparent women are the truly dangerous. There was one on ship–board [Mandeville likes to say that; he has just returned from a little tour in Europe, and he quite often begins his remarks with "on the ship going over; "the Young Lady declares that he has a sort of roll in his chair, when he says it, that makes her sea–sick] who was the most innocent, artless, guileless, natural bunch of lace and feathers you ever saw; she was all candor and helplessness and dependence; she sang like a nightingale, and talked like a nun. There never was such simplicity. There was n't a sounding–line on board that would have gone to the bottom of her soulful eyes. But she managed the captain and all the officers, and controlled the ship as if she had been the helm. All the passengers were waiting on her, fetching this and that for her comfort, inquiring of her health, talking about her genuineness, and exhibiting as much anxiety to get her ashore in safety, as if she had been about to knight them all and give them a castle apiece when they came to land.

THE MISTRESS. What harm? It shows what I have always said, that the service of a noble woman is the most ennobling influence for men.

MANDEVILLE. If she is noble, and not a mere manager. I watched this woman to see if she would ever do anything for any one else. She never did.

THE FIRE–TENDER. Did you ever see her again? I presume Mandeville has introduced her here for some purpose.

MANDEVILLE. No purpose. But we did see her on the Rhine; she was the most disgusted traveler, and seemed to be in very ill humor with her maid. I judged that her happiness depended upon establishing controlling relations with all about her. On this Rhine boat, to be sure, there was reason for disgust. And that reminds me of a remark that was made.

THE YOUNG LADY. Oh!

MANDEVILLE. When we got aboard at Mayence we were conscious of a dreadful odor somewhere; as it was a foggy morning, we could see no cause of it, but concluded it was from something on the wharf. The fog lifted, and we got under way, but the odor traveled with us, and increased. We went to every part of the vessel to avoid it, but in vain. It occasionally reached us in great waves of disagreeableness. We had heard of the odors of the towns on the Rhine, but we had no idea that the entire stream was infected. It was intolerable.

The day was lovely, and the passengers stood about on deck holding their noses and admiring the scenery. You might see a row of them leaning over the side, gazing up at some old ruin or ivied crag, entranced with the romance of the situation, and all holding their noses with thumb and finger. The sweet Rhine! By and by somebody discovered that the odor came from a pile of cheese on the forward deck, covered with a canvas; it seemed that the Rhinelanders are so fond of it that they take it with them when they travel. If there should ever be war between us and Germany, the borders of the Rhine would need no other defense from American soldiers than a barricade of this cheese. I went to the stern of the steamboat to tell a stout American traveler what was the origin of the odor he had been trying to dodge all the morning. He looked more disgusted than before, when he heard that it was cheese; but his only reply was: "It must be a merciful God who can forgive a smell like that!"

II

Backlog Studies

The above is introduced here in order to illustrate the usual effect of an anecdote on conversation. Commonly it kills it. That talk must be very well in hand, and under great headway, that an anecdote thrown in front of will not pitch off the track and wreck. And it makes little difference what the anecdote is; a poor one depresses the spirits, and casts a gloom over the company; a good one begets others, and the talkers go to telling stories; which is very good entertainment in moderation, but is not to be mistaken for that unwearying flow of argument, quaint remark, humorous color, and sprightly interchange of sentiments and opinions, called conversation.

The reader will perceive that all hope is gone here of deciding whether Herbert could have written Tennyson's poems, or whether Tennyson could have dug as much money out of the Heliogabalus Lode as Herbert did. The more one sees of life, I think the impression deepens that men, after all, play about the parts assigned them, according to their mental and moral gifts, which are limited and preordained, and that their entrances and exits are governed by a law no less certain because it is hidden. Perhaps nobody ever accomplishes all that he feels lies in him to do; but nearly every one who tries his powers touches the walls of his being occasionally, and learns about how far to attempt to spring. There are no impossibilities to youth and inexperience; but when a person has tried several times to reach high C and been coughed down, he is quite content to go down among the chorus. It is only the fools who keep straining at high C all their lives.

Mandeville here began to say that that reminded him of something that happened when he was on the

But Herbert cut in with the observation that no matter what a man's single and several capacities and talents might be, he is controlled by his own mysterious individuality, which is what metaphysicians call the substance, all else being the mere accidents of the man. And this is the reason that we cannot with any certainty tell what any person will do or amount to, for, while we know his talents and abilities, we do not know the resulting whole, which is he himself. THE FIRE–TENDER. So if you could take all the first–class qualities that we admire in men and women, and put them together into one being, you wouldn't be sure of the result?

HERBERT. Certainly not. You would probably have a monster. It takes a cook of long experience, with the best materials, to make a dish " taste good;" and the "taste good" is the indefinable essence, the resulting balance or harmony which makes man or woman agreeable or beautiful or effective in the world.

THE YOUNG LADY. That must be the reason why novelists fail so lamentably in almost all cases in creating good characters. They put in real traits, talents, dispositions, but the result of the synthesis is something that never was seen on earth before.

THE FIRE–TENDER. Oh, a good character in fiction is an inspiration. We admit this in poetry. It is as true of such creations as Colonel Newcome, and Ethel, and Beatrix Esmond. There is no patchwork about them.

THE YOUNG LADY. Why was n't Thackeray ever inspired to create a noble woman?

THE FIRE–TENDER. That is the standing conundrum with all the women. They will not accept Ethel Newcome even. Perhaps we shall have to admit that Thackeray was a writer for men.

HERBERT. Scott and the rest had drawn so many perfect women that Thackeray thought it was time for a real one.

THE MISTRESS. That's ill–natured. Thackeray did, however, make ladies. If he had depicted, with his searching pen, any of us just as we are, I doubt if we should have liked it much.

MANDEVILLE. That's just it. Thackeray never pretended to make ideals, and if the best novel is an idealization of human nature, then he was not the best novelist. When I was crossing the Channel

THE MISTRESS. Oh dear, if we are to go to sea again, Mandeville, I move we have in the nuts and apples, and talk about our friends.

III

There is this advantage in getting back to a wood–fire on the hearth, that you return to a kind of simplicity; you can scarcely imagine any one being stiffly conventional in front of it. It thaws out formality, and puts the company who sit around it into easy attitudes of mind and body,—lounging attitudes,—Herbert said.

And this brought up the subject of culture in America, especially as to manner. The backlog period having passed, we are beginning to have in society people of the cultured manner, as it is called, or polished bearing, in which the polish is the most noticeable thing about the man. Not the courtliness, the easy simplicity of the old–school gentleman, in whose presence the milkmaid was as much at her ease as the countess, but something far finer than this. These are the people of unruffled demeanor, who never forget it for a moment, and never let you forget it. Their presence is a constant rebuke to society. They are never "jolly;" their laugh is never anything more than a well–bred smile; they are never betrayed into any enthusiasm. Enthusiasm is a sign of inexperience, of ignorance, of want of culture. They never lose themselves in any cause; they never heartily praise any man or woman or book; they are superior to all tides of feeling and all outbursts of passion. They are not even shocked at vulgarity. They are simply indifferent. They are calm, visibly calm, painfully calm; and it is not the eternal, majestic calmness of the Sphinx either, but a rigid, self–conscious repression. You would like to put a bent pin in their chair when they are about calmly to sit down.

A sitting hen on her nest is calm, but hopeful; she has faith that her eggs are not china. These people appear to be sitting on china eggs. Perfect culture has refined all blood, warmth, flavor, out of them. We admire them without envy. They are too beautiful in their manners to be either prigs or snobs. They are at once our models and our despair. They are properly careful of themselves as models, for they know that if they should break, society would become a scene of mere animal confusion.

MANDEVILLE. I think that the best–bred people in the world are the English.

THE YOUNG LADY. You mean at home.

MANDEVILLE. That's where I saw them. There is no nonsense about a cultivated English man or woman. They express themselves sturdily and naturally, and with no subservience to the opinions of others. There's a sort of hearty sincerity about them that I like. Ages of culture on the island have gone deeper than the surface, and they have simpler and more natural manners than we. There is something good in the full, round tones of their voices.

HERBERT. Did you ever get into a diligence with a growling English– man who had n't secured the place he wanted?

Backlog Studies

[Mandeville once spent a week in London, riding about on the tops of omnibuses.]

THE MISTRESS. Did you ever see an English exquisite at the San Carlo, and hear him cry "Bwavo"?

MANDEVILLE. At any rate, he acted out his nature, and was n't afraid to.

THE FIRE-TENDER. I think Mandeville is right, for once. The men of the best culture in England, in the middle and higher social classes, are what you would call good fellows,—easy and simple in manner, enthusiastic on occasion, and decidedly not cultivated into the smooth calmness of indifference which some Americans seem to regard as the sine qua non of good breeding. Their position is so assured that they do not need that lacquer of calmness of which we were speaking.

THE YOUNG LADY. Which is different from the manner acquired by those who live a great deal in American hotels?

THE MISTRESS. Or the Washington manner?

HERBERT. The last two are the same.

THE FIRE-TENDER. Not exactly. You think you can always tell if a man has learned his society carriage of a dancing-master. Well, you cannot always tell by a person's manner whether he is a habitui of hotels or of Washington. But these are distinct from the perfect polish and politeness of indifferentism.

IV

Daylight disenchants. It draws one from the fireside, and dissipates the idle illusions of conversation, except under certain conditions. Let us say that the conditions are: a house in the country, with some forest trees near, and a few evergreens, which are Christmas-trees all winter long, fringed with snow, glistening with ice-pendants, cheerful by day and grotesque by night; a snow-storm beginning out of a dark sky, falling in a soft profusion that fills all the air, its dazzling whiteness making a light near at hand, which is quite lost in the distant darkling spaces.

Backlog Studies

If one begins to watch the swirling flakes and crystals, he soon gets an impression of infinity of resources that he can have from nothing else so powerfully, except it be from Adirondack gnats. Nothing makes one feel at home like a great snow–storm. Our intelligent cat will quit the fire and sit for hours in the low window, watching the falling snow with a serious and contented air. His thoughts are his own, but he is in accord with the subtlest agencies of Nature; on such a day he is charged with enough electricity to run a telegraphic battery, if it could be utilized. The connection between thought and electricity has not been exactly determined, but the cat is mentally very alert in certain conditions of the atmosphere. Feasting his eyes on the beautiful out–doors does not prevent his attention to the slightest noise in the wainscot. And the snow–storm brings content, but not stupidity, to all the rest of the household.

I can see Mandeville now, rising from his armchair and swinging his long arms as he strides to the window, and looks out and up, with, "Well, I declare!" Herbert is pretending to read Herbert Spencer's tract on the philosophy of style but he loses much time in looking at the Young Lady, who is writing a letter, holding her portfolio in her lap,—one of her everlasting letters to one of her fifty everlasting friends. She is one of the female patriots who save the post–office department from being a disastrous loss to the treasury. Herbert is thinking of the great radical difference in the two sexes, which legislation will probably never change; that leads a woman always, to write letters on her lap and a man on a table,—a distinction which is commended to the notice of the anti–suffragists.

The Mistress, in a pretty little breakfast–cap, is moving about the room with a feather–duster, whisking invisible dust from the picture– frames, and talking with the Parson, who has just come in, and is thawing the snow from his boots on the hearth. The Parson says the thermometer is 15deg., and going down; that there is a snowdrift across the main church entrance three feet high, and that the house looks as if it had gone into winter quarters, religion and all. There were only ten persons at the conference meeting last night, and seven of those were women; he wonders how many weather–proof Christians there are in the parish, anyhow.

The Fire–Tender is in the adjoining library, pretending to write; but it is a poor day for ideas. He has written his wife's name about eleven hundred times, and cannot get any farther. He hears the Mistress tell the Parson that she believes he is trying to write a lecture on the Celtic Influence in Literature. The Parson says that it is a first–rate subject, if there were any such influence, and asks why he does n't take a shovel and make a path to the gate. Mandeville says that, by George! he himself should like no better fun, but it wouldn't look well for a visitor to do it. The Fire–Tender, not to be disturbed by this sort of chaff, keeps on writing his wife's name.

Then the Parson and the Mistress fall to talking about the soup–relief, and about old Mrs. Grumples in Pig Alley, who had a present of one of Stowe's Illustrated Self–Acting Bibles on Christmas, when she had n't coal enough in the house to heat her gruel; and about a family behind the church, a widow and six little children and three dogs; and he did n't believe that any of them had known what it was to be warm in three weeks, and as to food, the woman said, she could hardly beg cold victuals enough to keep the dogs alive.

The Mistress slipped out into the kitchen to fill a basket with provisions and send it somewhere; and when the Fire–Tender brought in a new forestick, Mandeville, who always wants to talk, and had been sitting drumming his feet and drawing deep sighs, attacked him.

MANDEVILLE. Speaking about culture and manners, did you ever notice how extremes meet, and that the savage bears himself very much like the sort of cultured persons we were talking of last night?

THE FIRE–TENDER. In what respect?

MANDEVILLE. Well, you take the North American Indian. He is never interested in anything, never surprised at anything. He has by nature that calmness and indifference which your people of culture have acquired. If he should go into literature as a critic, he would scalp and tomahawk with the same emotionless composure, and he would do nothing else.

THE FIRE–TENDER. Then you think the red man is a born gentleman of the highest breeding?

MANDEVILLE. I think he is calm.

THE FIRE–TENDER. How is it about the war–path and all that?

31

MANDEVILLE. Oh, these studiously calm and cultured people may have malice underneath. It takes them to give the most effective "little digs;" they know how to stick in the pine—splinters and set fire to them.

HERBERT. But there is more in Mandeville's idea. You bring a red man into a picture—gallery, or a city full of fine architecture, or into a drawing—room crowded with objects of art and beauty, and he is apparently insensible to them all. Now I have seen country people,— and by country people I don't mean people necessarily who live in the country, for everything is mixed in these days,—some of the best people in the world, intelligent, honest, sincere, who acted as the Indian would.

THE MISTRESS. Herbert, if I did n't know you were cynical, I should say you were snobbish.

HERBERT. Such people think it a point of breeding never to speak of anything in your house, nor to appear to notice it, however beautiful it may be; even to slyly glance around strains their notion of etiquette. They are like the countryman who confessed afterwards that he could hardly keep from laughing at one of Yankee Hill's entertainments,

THE YOUNG LADY. Do you remember those English people at our house in Flushing last summer, who pleased us all so much with their apparent delight in everything that was artistic or tasteful, who explored the rooms and looked at everything, and were so interested? I suppose that Herbert's country relations, many of whom live in the city, would have thought it very ill—bred.

MANDEVILLE. It's just as I said. The English, the best of them, have become so civilized that they express themselves, in speech and action, naturally, and are not afraid of their emotions.

THE PARSON. I wish Mandeville would travel more, or that he had stayed at home. It's wonderful what a fit of Atlantic sea—sickness will do for a man's judgment and cultivation. He is prepared to pronounce on art, manners, all kinds of culture. There is more nonsense talked about culture than about anything else.

HERBERT. The Parson reminds me of an American country minister I once met walking through the Vatican. You could n't impose upon him with any rubbish; he tested everything by the standards of his native place, and there was little that could bear the test. He had the sly air of a man who could not be deceived, and he went about with his mouth in a pucker of incredulity. There is nothing so placid as rustic conceit. There was something very enjoyable about his calm superiority to all the treasures of art.

MANDEVILLE. And the Parson reminds me of another American minister, a consul in an Italian city, who said he was going up to Rome to have a thorough talk with the Pope, and give him a piece of his mind. Ministers seem to think that is their business. They serve it in such small pieces in order to make it go round.

THE PARSON. Mandeville is an infidel. Come, let's have some music; nothing else will keep him in good humor till lunch–time.

THE MISTRESS. What shall it be?

THE PARSON. Give us the larghetto from Beethoven's second symphony.

The Young Lady puts aside her portfolio. Herbert looks at the young lady. The Parson composes himself for critical purposes. Mandeville settles himself in a chair and stretches his long legs nearly into the fire, remarking that music takes the tangles out of him.

After the piece is finished, lunch is announced. It is still snowing.

FOURTH STUDY

It is difficult to explain the attraction which the uncanny and even the horrible have for most minds. I have seen a delicate woman half fascinated, but wholly disgusted, by one of the most unseemly of reptiles, vulgarly known as the "blowing viper" of the Alleghanies. She would look at it, and turn away with irresistible shuddering and the utmost loathing, and yet turn to look at it again and again, only to experience the same spasm of disgust. In spite of her aversion, she must have relished the sort of electric mental shock that the sight gave her.

I can no more account for the fascination for us of the stories of ghosts and "appearances," and those weird tales in which the dead are the chief characters; nor tell why we should fall into converse about them when the winter evenings are far spent, the embers are glazing over on the hearth, and the listener begins to hear the eerie noises in the house. At such times one's dreams become of importance, and people like to tell them and dwell upon them, as if they were a link between the known and unknown, and could give us a clew to that ghostly region which in certain states of the mind we feel to be more real than that we see.

Recently, when we were, so to say, sitting around the borders of the supernatural late at night, MANDEVILLE related a dream of his which he assured us was true in every particular, and it interested us so much that we asked him to write it out. In doing so he has curtailed it, and to my mind shorn it of some of its more vivid and picturesque features. He might have worked it up with more art, and given it a finish which the narration now lacks, but I think best to insert it in its simplicity. It seems to me that it may properly be called,

A NEW "VISION OF SIN"

In the winter of 1850 I was a member of one of the leading colleges of this country. I was in moderate circumstances pecuniarily, though I was perhaps better furnished with less fleeting riches than many others. I was an incessant and indiscriminate reader of books. For the solid sciences I had no particular fancy, but with mental modes and habits, and especially with the eccentric and fantastic in the intellectual and spiritual operations, I was tolerably familiar. All the literature of the supernatural was as real to me as the laboratory of the chemist, where I saw the continual struggle of material substances to evolve themselves into more volatile, less palpable and coarse forms. My imagination, naturally vivid, stimulated by such repasts, nearly mastered me. At times I could scarcely tell where the material ceased and the immaterial began (if I may so express it); so that once and again I walked, as it seemed, from the solid earth onward upon an impalpable plain, where I heard the same voices, I think, that Joan of Arc heard call to her in the garden at Domremy. She was inspired, however, while I only lacked exercise. I do not mean this in any literal sense; I only describe a state of mind. I was at this time of spare habit, and nervous, excitable temperament. I was ambitious, proud, and extremely sensitive. I cannot deny that I had seen something of the world, and had contracted about the average bad habits of young men who have the sole care of themselves, and rather bungle the matter. It is necessary to this relation to admit that I had seen a trifle more of what is called life than a young man ought to see, but at this period I was not only sick of my experience, but my habits were as correct as those of any Pharisee in our college, and we had some very favorable specimens of that ancient sect.

Nor can I deny that at this period of my life I was in a peculiar mental condition. I well remember an illustration of it. I sat writing late one night, copying a prize essay,—a merely manual task, leaving my thoughts free. It was in June, a sultry night, and about midnight a wind arose, pouring in through the open windows, full of mournful reminiscence, not of this, but of other summers, —the same wind that De Quincey heard at noonday in midsummer blowing through the room where he stood, a mere boy, by the side of his dead sister,— —a wind centuries old. As I wrote on mechanically, I became conscious of a presence in the room, though I did not lift my eyes from the paper on which I wrote. Gradually I came to know that my grandmother—dead so long ago that I laughed at the idea—was in the room. She stood beside her old-fashioned spinning-wheel, and quite near me. She wore a plain muslin cap with a high puff in the crown, a short woolen gown, a white and blue checked apron, and shoes with heels. She did not regard me, but stood facing the wheel, with the left hand near the spindle, holding lightly between the thumb and forefinger the white roll of wool which was being spun and twisted on it. In her right hand she held a small stick. I heard the sharp click of this against the spokes of the wheel, then the hum of the wheel, the buzz of the spindles as the twisting yarn was teased by the whirl of its point, then a step backwards, a pause, a step forward and the running of the yarn upon the spindle, and again a backward step, the drawing out of the roll and the droning and hum of the wheel, most mournfully hopeless sound that ever fell on mortal ear. Since childhood it has haunted me. All this time I wrote, and I could hear distinctly the scratching of the pen upon the paper. But she stood behind me (why I did not turn my head I never knew), pacing backward and forward by the spinning-wheel, just as I had a hundred times seen her in childhood in the old kitchen on drowsy summer afternoons. And I heard the step, the buzz and whirl of the spindle, and the monotonous and dreary hum of the mournful wheel. Whether her face was ashy pale and looked as if it might crumble at the touch, and the border of her white cap trembled in the June wind that blew, I cannot say, for I tell you I did NOT see her. But I know she was there, spinning yarn that had been knit into hose years and years ago by our fireside. For I was in full possession of my faculties, and never copied more neatly and legibly any manuscript than I did the one that night. And there the phantom (I use the word out of deference to a public prejudice on this subject) most persistently remained until my task was finished, and, closing the portfolio, I abruptly rose. Did I see anything? That is a silly and ignorant question. Could I see the wind which had now risen stronger, and drove a few cloud–scuds across the sky, filling the night, somehow, with a longing that was not altogether born of reminiscence?

In the winter following, in January, I made an effort to give up the use of tobacco,—a habit in which I was confirmed, and of which I have nothing more to say than this: that I should attribute to it almost all the sin and misery in the world, did I not remember that the old Romans attained a very considerable state of corruption without the assistance of the Virginia plant.

On the night of the third day of my abstinence, rendered more nervous and excitable than usual by the privation, I retired late, and later still I fell into an uneasy sleep, and thus into a dream, vivid, illuminated, more real than any event of my life. I was at home, and fell sick. The illness developed into a fever, and then a delirium set in, not an intellectual blank, but a misty and most delicious wandering in places of incomparable beauty. I learned subsequently that our regular physician was not certain to finish me, when a consultation was called, which did the business. I have the satisfaction of knowing that they were of the proper school. I lay sick for three days.

On the morning of the fourth, at sunrise, I died. The sensation was not unpleasant. It was not a sudden shock. I passed out of my body as one would walk from the door of his house. There the body lay,—a blank, so far as I was concerned, and only interesting to me as I was rather entertained with watching the respect paid to it. My friends stood about the bedside, regarding me (as they seemed to suppose), while I, in a different part of the room, could hardly repress a smile at their mistake, solemnized as they were, and I too, for that matter, by my recent demise. A sensation (the word you see is material and inappropriate) of etherealization and imponderability pervaded me, and I was not sorry to get rid of such a dull, slow mass as I now perceived myself to be, lying there on the bed. When I speak of my death, let me be understood to say that there was no change, except that I passed out of my body and floated to the top of a bookcase in the corner of the room, from which I looked down. For a moment I was interested to see my person from the outside, but thereafter I was quite indifferent to the body. I was now simply soul. I seemed to be a globe, impalpable, transparent, about six inches in diameter. I saw and heard everything as before. Of course, matter was no obstacle to me, and I went easily and quickly wherever I willed to go. There was none of that tedious process of communicating my wishes to the nerves, and from them to the muscles. I simply resolved to be at a particular place, and I was there. It was better than the telegraph.

Backlog Studies

It seemed to have been intimated to me at my death (birth I half incline to call it) that I could remain on this earth for four weeks after my decease, during which time I could amuse myself as I chose.

I chose, in the first place, to see myself decently buried, to stay by myself to the last, and attend my own funeral for once. As most of those referred to in this true narrative are still living, I am forbidden to indulge in personalities, nor shall I dare to say exactly how my death affected my friends, even the home circle. Whatever others did, I sat up with myself and kept awake. I saw the "pennies" used instead of the "quarters" which I should have preferred. I saw myself "laid out," a phrase that has come to have such a slang meaning that I smile as I write it. When the body was put into the coffin, I took my place on the lid.

I cannot recall all the details, and they are commonplace besides. The funeral took place at the church. We all rode thither in carriages, and I, not fancying my place in mine, rode on the outside with the undertaker, whom I found to be a good deal more jolly than he looked to be. The coffin was placed in front of the pulpit when we arrived. I took my station on the pulpit cushion, from which elevation I had an admirable view of all the ceremonies, and could hear the sermon. How distinctly I remember the services. I think I could even at this distance write out the sermon. The tune sung was of—the usual country selection,—Mount Vernon. I recall the text. I was rather flattered by the tribute paid to me, and my future was spoken of gravely and as kindly as possible,—indeed, with remarkable charity, considering that the minister was not aware of my presence. I used to beat him at chess, and I thought, even then, of the last game; for, however solemn the occasion might be to others, it was not so to me. With what interest I watched my kinsfolks, and neighbors as they filed past for the last look! I saw, and I remember, who pulled a long face for the occasion and who exhibited genuine sadness. I learned with the most dreadful certainty what people really thought of me. It was a revelation never forgotten.

Several particular acquaintances of mine were talking on the steps as we passed out.

"Well, old Starr's gone up. Sudden, was n't it? He was a first–rate fellow."

"Yes, queer about some things; but he had some mighty good streaks," said another. And so they ran on.

Backlog Studies

Streaks! So that is the reputation one gets during twenty years of life in this world. Streaks!

After the funeral I rode home with the family. It was pleasanter than the ride down, though it seemed sad to my relations. They did not mention me, however, and I may remark, that although I stayed about home for a week, I never heard my name mentioned by any of the family. Arrived at home, the tea–kettle was put on and supper got ready. This seemed to lift the gloom a little, and under the influence of the tea they brightened up and gradually got more cheerful. They discussed the sermon and the singing, and the mistake of the sexton in digging the grave in the wrong place, and the large congregation. From the mantel–piece I watched the group. They had waffles for supper,—of which I had been exceedingly fond, but now I saw them disappear without a sigh.

For the first day or two of my sojourn at home I was here and there at all the neighbors, and heard a good deal about my life and character, some of which was not very pleasant, but very wholesome, doubtless, for me to hear. At the expiration of a week this amusement ceased to be such for I ceased to be talked of. I realized the fact that I was dead and gone.

By an act of volition I found myself back at college. I floated into my own room, which was empty. I went to the room of my two warmest friends, whose friendship I was and am yet assured of. As usual, half a dozen of our set were lounging there. A game of whist was just commencing. I perched on a bust of Dante on the top of the book–shelves, where I could see two of the hands and give a good guess at a third. My particular friend Timmins was just shuffling the cards.

"Be hanged if it is n't lonesome without old Starr. Did you cut? I should like to see him lounge in now with his pipe, and with feet on the mantel–piece proceed to expound on the duplex functions of the soul."

"There—misdeal," said his vis-,a–vis. "Hope there's been no misdeal for old Starr."

"Spades, did you say?" the talk ran on, "never knew Starr was sickly."

"No more was he; stouter than you are, and as brave and plucky as he was strong. By George, fellows,—how we do get cut down! Last term little Stubbs, and now one of the best fellows in the class."

"How suddenly he did pop off,—one for game, honors easy,—he was good for the Spouts' Medal this year, too."

"Remember the joke he played on Prof. A., freshman year? "asked another.

"Remember he borrowed ten dollars of me about that time," said Timmins's partner, gathering the cards for a new deal.

"Guess he is the only one who ever did," retorted some one.

And so the talk went on, mingled with whist–talk, reminiscent of me, not all exactly what I would have chosen to go into my biography, but on the whole kind and tender, after the fashion of the boys. At least I was in their thoughts, and I could see was a good deal regretted,—so I passed a very pleasant evening. Most of those present were of my society, and wore crape on their badges, and all wore the usual crape on the left arm. I learned that the following afternoon a eulogy would be delivered on me in the chapel.

The eulogy was delivered before members of our society and others, the next afternoon, in the chapel. I need not say that I was present. Indeed, I was perched on the desk within reach of the speaker's hand. The apotheosis was pronounced by my most intimate friend, Timmins, and I must say he did me ample justice. He never was accustomed to "draw it very mild" (to use a vulgarism which I dislike) when he had his head, and on this occasion he entered into the matter with the zeal of a true friend, and a young man who never expected to have another occasion to sing a public "In Memoriam." It made my hair stand on end,—metaphorically, of course. From my childhood I had been extremely precocious. There were anecdotes of preternatural brightness, picked up, Heaven knows where, of my eagerness to learn, of my adventurous, chivalrous young soul, and of my arduous struggles with chill penury, which was not able (as it appeared) to repress my rage, until I entered this institution, of which I had been ornament, pride, cynosure, and fair promising bud blasted while yet its fragrance was mingled with the dew of its youth. Once launched upon my college days, Timmins went on with all sails spread. I had, as it were, to hold on to the pulpit cushion. Latin, Greek, the old literatures, I was perfect master of; all history was merely a light repast to me; mathematics I glanced at, and it disappeared; in the clouds of modern philosophy I was wrapped but not obscured; over the field of light literature I familiarly roamed as the honey–bee over the wide fields of clover which blossom white in the Junes of this world! My life was pure, my character spotless, my name was inscribed among the names of those deathless few who were not born to die!

It was a noble eulogy, and I felt before he finished, though I had misgivings at the beginning, that I deserved it all. The effect on the audience was a little different. They said it was a "strong" oration, and I think Timmins got more credit by it than I did. After the performance they stood about the chapel, talking in a subdued tone, and seemed to be a good deal impressed by what they had heard, or perhaps by thoughts of the departed. At least they all soon went over to Austin's and called for beer. My particular friends called for it twice. Then they all lit pipes. The old grocery keeper was good enough to say that I was no fool, if I did go off owing him four dollars. To the credit of human nature, let me here record that the fellows were touched by this remark reflecting upon my memory, and immediately made up a purse and paid the bill,—that is, they told the old man to charge it over to them. College boys are rich in credit and the possibilities of life.

It is needless to dwell upon the days I passed at college during this probation. So far as I could see, everything went on as if I were there, or had never been there. I could not even see the place where I had dropped out of the ranks. Occasionally I heard my name, but I must say that four weeks was quite long enough to stay in a world that had pretty much forgotten me. There is no great satisfaction in being dragged up to light now and then, like an old letter. The case was somewhat different with the people with whom I had boarded. They were relations of mine, and I often saw them weep, and they talked of me a good deal at twilight and Sunday nights, especially the youngest one, Carrie, who was handsomer than any one I knew, and not much older than I. I never used to imagine that she cared particularly for me, nor would she have done so, if I had lived, but death brought with it a sort of sentimental regret, which, with the help of a daguerreotype, she nursed into quite a little passion. I spent most of my time there, for it was more congenial than the college.

But time hastened. The last sand of probation leaked out of the glass. One day, while Carrie played (for me, though she knew it not) one of Mendelssohn's "songs without words," I suddenly, yet gently, without self–effort or volition, moved from the house, floated in the air, rose higher, higher, by an easy, delicious, exultant, yet inconceivably rapid motion. The ecstasy of that triumphant flight! Groves, trees, houses, the landscape, dimmed, faded, fled away beneath me. Upward mounting, as on angels' wings, with no effort, till the earth hung beneath me a round black ball swinging, remote, in the universal ether. Upward mounting, till the earth, no longer bathed in the sun's rays, went out to my sight, disappeared in the blank. Constellations, before seen from afar, I sailed among. Stars, too remote for shining on earth, I neared, and found to be round globes flying through space with a velocity only equaled by my own. New worlds continually opened on my sight; newfields of everlasting space opened and closed behind me.

For days and days—it seemed a mortal forever—I mounted up the great heavens, whose everlasting doors swung wide. How the worlds and systems, stars, constellations, neared me, blazed and flashed in splendor, and fled away! At length,—was it not a thousand years?—I saw before me, yet afar off, a wall, the rocky bourn of that country whence travelers come not back, a battlement wider than I could guess, the height of which I could not see, the depth of which was infinite. As I approached, it shone with a splendor never yet beheld on earth. Its solid substance was built of jewels the rarest, and stones of priceless value. It seemed like one solid stone, and yet all the colors of the rainbow were contained in it. The ruby, the diamond, the emerald, the carbuncle, the topaz, the amethyst, the sapphire; of them the wall was built up in harmonious combination. So brilliant was it that all the space I floated in was full of the splendor. So mild was it and so translucent, that I could look for miles into its clear depths.

Rapidly nearing this heavenly battlement, an immense niche was disclosed in its solid face. The floor was one large ruby. Its sloping sides were of pearl. Before I was aware I stood within the brilliant recess. I say I stood there, for I was there bodily, in my habit as I lived; how, I cannot explain. Was it the resurrection of the body? Before me rose, a thousand feet in height, a wonderful gate of flashing diamond. Beside it sat a venerable man, with long white beard, a robe of light gray, ancient sandals, and a golden key hanging by a cord from his waist. In the serene beauty of his noble features I saw justice and mercy had met and were reconciled. I cannot describe the majesty of his bearing or the benignity of his appearance. It is needless to say that I stood before St. Peter, who sits at the Celestial Gate.

I humbly approached, and begged admission. St. Peter arose, and regarded me kindly, yet inquiringly.

"What is your name? " asked he, "and from what place do you come?"

Backlog Studies

I answered, and, wishing to give a name well known, said I was from Washington, United States. He looked doubtful, as if he had never heard the name before.

"Give me," said he, "a full account of your whole life."

I felt instantaneously that there was no concealment possible; all disguise fell away, and an unknown power forced me to speak absolute and exact truth. I detailed the events of my life as well as I could, and the good man was not a little affected by the recital of my early trials, poverty, and temptation. It did not seem a very good life when spread out in that presence, and I trembled as I proceeded; but I plead youth, inexperience, and bad examples.

Have you been accustomed," he said, after a time, rather sadly, "to break the Sabbath?"

I told him frankly that I had been rather lax in that matter, especially at college. I often went to sleep in the chapel on Sunday, when I was not reading some entertaining book. He then asked who the preacher was, and when I told him, he remarked that I was not so much to blame as he had supposed.

"Have you," he went on, "ever stolen, or told any lie?"

I was able to say no, except admitting as to the first, usual college "conveyances," and as to the last, an occasional "blinder" to the professors. He was gracious enough to say that these could be overlooked as incident to the occasion.

"Have you ever been dissipated, living riotously and keeping late hours?"

"Yes."

This also could be forgiven me as an incident of youth.

"Did you ever," he went on, "commit the crime of using intoxicating drinks as a beverage?"

I answered that I had never been a habitual drinker, that I had never been what was called a "moderate drinker," that I had never gone to a bar and drank alone; but that I had been accustomed, in company with other young men, on convivial occasions to taste the pleasures of the flowing bowl, sometimes to excess, but that I had also tasted the pains of it, and for months before my demise had refrained from liquor altogether. The holy man looked grave, but, after reflection, said this might also be overlooked in a young man.

"What," continued he, in tones still more serious, "has been your conduct with regard to the other sex?"

I fell upon my knees in a tremor of fear. I pulled from my bosom a little book like the one Leperello exhibits in the opera of "Don Giovanni." There, I said, was a record of my flirtation and inconstancy. I waited long for the decision, but it came in mercy.

"Rise," he cried; "young men will be young men, I suppose. We shall forgive this also to your youth and penitence."

"Your examination is satisfactory, he informed me," after a pause; "you can now enter the abodes of the happy."

Joy leaped within me. We approached the gate. The key turned in the lock. The gate swung noiselessly on its hinges a little open. Out flashed upon me unknown splendors. What I saw in that momentary gleam I shall never whisper in mortal ears. I stood upon the threshold, just about to enter.

"Stop! one moment," exclaimed St. Peter, laying his hand on my shoulder; "I have one more question to ask you."

I turned toward him.

"Young man, did you ever use tobacco?"

"I both smoked and chewed in my lifetime," I faltered, "but..."

"THEN TO HELL WITH YOU!" he shouted in a voice of thunder.

Instantly the gate closed without noise, and I was flung, hurled, from the battlement, down! down! down! Faster and faster I sank in a dizzy, sickening whirl into an unfathomable space of gloom. The light faded. Dampness and darkness were round about me. As before, for days and days I rose exultant in the light, so now forever I sank into thickening darkness,—and yet not darkness, but a pale, ashy light more fearful.

In the dimness, I at length discovered a wall before me. It ran up and down and on either hand endlessly into the night. It was solid, black, terrible in its frowning massiveness.

Straightway I alighted at the gate,—a dismal crevice hewn into the dripping rock. The gate was wide open, and there sat–I knew him at once; who does not?—the Arch Enemy of mankind. He cocked his eye at me in an impudent, low, familiar manner that disgusted me. I saw that I was not to be treated like a gentleman.

"Well, young man," said he, rising, with a queer grin on his face," what are you sent here for?

"For using tobacco," I replied.

"Ho!" shouted he in a jolly manner, peculiar to devils, "that's what most of 'em are sent here for now."

Without more ado, he called four lesser imps, who ushered me within. What a dreadful plain lay before me! There was a vast city laid out in regular streets, but there were no houses. Along the streets were places of torment and torture exceedingly ingenious and disagreeable. For miles and miles, it seemed, I followed my conductors through these horrors, Here was a deep vat of burning tar. Here were rows of fiery ovens. I noticed several immense caldron kettles of boiling oil, upon the rims of which little devils sat, with pitchforks in hand, and poked down the helpless victims who floundered in the liquid. But I forbear to go into unseemly details. The whole scene is as vivid in my mind as any earthly landscape.

After an hour's walk my tormentors halted before the mouth of an oven,—a furnace heated seven times, and now roaring with flames. They grasped me, one hold of each hand and foot. Standing before the blazing mouth, they, with a swing, and a "one, two, THREE...."

I again assure the reader that in this narrative I have set down nothing that was not actually dreamed, and much, very much of this wonderful vision I have been obliged to omit.

Haec fabula docet: It is dangerous for a young man to leave off the use of tobacco.

FIFTH STUDY

I

I wish I could fitly celebrate the joyousness of the New England winter. Perhaps I could if I more thoroughly believed in it. But skepticism comes in with the south wind. When that begins to blow, one feels the foundations of his belief breaking up. This is only another way of saying that it is more difficult, if it be not impossible, to freeze out orthodoxy, or any fixed notion, than it is to thaw it out; though it is a mere fancy to suppose that this is the reason why the martyrs, of all creeds, were burned at the stake. There is said to be a great relaxation in New England of the ancient strictness in the direction of toleration of opinion, called by some a lowering of the standard, and by others a raising of the banner of liberality; it might be an interesting inquiry how much this change is due to another change,—the softening of the New England winter and the shifting of the Gulf Stream. It is the fashion nowadays to refer almost everything to physical causes, and this hint is a gratuitous contribution to the science of metaphysical physics.

The hindrance to entering fully into the joyousness of a New England winter, except far inland among the mountains, is the south wind. It is a grateful wind, and has done more, I suspect, to demoralize society than any other. It is not necessary to remember that it filled the silken sails of Cleopatra's galley. It blows over New England every few days, and is in some portions of it the prevailing wind. That it brings the soft clouds, and sometimes continues long enough to almost deceive the expectant buds of the fruit trees, and to tempt the robin from the secluded evergreen copses, may be nothing; but it takes the tone out of the mind, and engenders discontent, making one long for the tropics; it feeds the weakened imagination on palm—leaves and the lotus. Before we know it we become demoralized, and shrink from the tonic of the sudden change to sharp weather, as the steamed hydropathic patient does from the plunge. It is the insidious temptation that assails us when we are braced up to profit by the invigorating rigor of winter.

Perhaps the influence of the four great winds on character is only a fancied one; but it is evident on temperament, which is not altogether a matter of temperature, although the good old deacon used to say, in his humble, simple way, that his third wife was a very good woman, but her "temperature was very different from that of the other two." The north wind is full of courage, and puts the stamina of endurance into a man, and it probably would into a woman too if there were a series of resolutions passed to that effect. The west wind is hopeful; it has promise and adventure in it, and is, except to Atlantic voyagers America—bound, the best wind that ever blew. The east wind is peevishness; it is mental rheumatism and grumbling, and curls one up in the chimney—corner like a cat. And if the chimney ever smokes, it smokes when the wind sits in that quarter. The south wind is full of longing and unrest, of effeminate suggestions of luxurious ease, and perhaps we might say of modern poetry,—at any rate, modern poetry needs a change of air. I am not sure but the south is the most powerful of the winds, because of its sweet persuasiveness. Nothing so stirs the blood in spring, when it comes up out of the tropical latitude; it makes men "longen to gon on pilgrimages."

I did intend to insert here a little poem (as it is quite proper to do in an essay) on the south wind, composed by the Young Lady Staying With Us, beginning,—

"Out of a drifting southern cloud My soul heard the night—bird cry,"

but it never got any farther than this. The Young Lady said it was exceedingly difficult to write the next two lines, because not only rhyme but meaning had to be procured. And this is true; anybody can write first lines, and that is probably the reason we have so many poems which seem to have been begun in just this way, that is, with a south—wind—longing without any thought in it, and it is very fortunate when there is not wind enough to finish them. This emotional poem, if I may so call it, was begun after Herbert went away. I liked it, and thought it was what is called "suggestive;" although I did not understand it, especially what the night—bird was; and I am afraid I hurt the Young Lady's feelings by asking her if she meant Herbert by the "night—bird,"—a very absurd suggestion about two unsentimental people. She said, "Nonsense;" but she afterwards told the Mistress that there were emotions that one could never put into words without the danger of being ridiculous; a profound truth. And yet I should not like to say that there is not a tender lonesomeness in love that can get comfort out of a night—bird in a cloud, if there be such a thing. Analysis is the death of sentiment.

But to return to the winds. Certain people impress us as the winds do. Mandeville never comes in that I do not feel a north–wind vigor and healthfulness in his cordial, sincere, hearty manner, and in his wholesome way of looking at things. The Parson, you would say, was the east wind, and only his intimates know that his peevishness is only a querulous humor. In the fair west wind I know the Mistress herself, full of hope, and always the first one to discover a bit of blue in a cloudy sky. It would not be just to apply what I have said of the south wind to any of our visitors, but it did blow a little while Herbert was here.

II

In point of pure enjoyment, with an intellectual sparkle in it, I suppose that no luxurious lounging on tropical isles set in tropical seas compares with the positive happiness one may have before a great woodfire (not two sticks laid crossways in a grate), with a veritable New England winter raging outside. In order to get the highest enjoyment, the faculties must be alert, and not be lulled into a mere recipient dullness. There are those who prefer a warm bath to a brisk walk in the inspiring air, where ten thousand keen influences minister to the sense of beauty and run along the excited nerves. There are, for instance, a sharpness of horizon outline and a delicacy of color on distant hills which are wanting in summer, and which convey to one rightly organized the keenest delight, and a refinement of enjoyment that is scarcely sensuous, not at all sentimental, and almost passing the intellectual line into the spiritual.

I was speaking to Mandeville about this, and he said that I was drawing it altogether too fine; that he experienced sensations of pleasure in being out in almost all weathers; that he rather liked to breast a north wind, and that there was a certain inspiration in sharp outlines and in a landscape in trim winter–quarters, with stripped trees, and, as it were, scudding through the season under bare poles; but that he must say that he preferred the weather in which he could sit on the fence by the wood–lot, with the spring sun on his back, and hear the stir of the leaves and the birds beginning their housekeeping.

A very pretty idea for Mandeville; and I fear he is getting to have private thoughts about the Young Lady. Mandeville naturally likes the robustness and sparkle of winter, and it has been a little suspicious to hear him express the hope that we shall have an early spring.

I wonder how many people there are in New England who know the glory and inspiration of a winter walk just before sunset, and that, too, not only on days of clear sky, when the west is aflame with a rosy color, which has no suggestion of languor or unsatisfied longing in it, but on dull days, when the sullen clouds hang about the horizon, full of threats of storm and the terrors of the gathering night. We are very busy with our own affairs, but there is always something going on out-doors worth looking at; and there is seldom an hour before sunset that has not some special attraction. And, besides, it puts one in the mood for the cheer and comfort of the open fire at home.

Probably if the people of New England could have a plebiscitum on their weather, they would vote against it, especially against winter. Almost no one speaks well of winter. And this suggests the idea that most people here were either born in the wrong place, or do not know what is best for them. I doubt if these grumblers would be any better satisfied, or would turn out as well, in the tropics. Everybody knows our virtues,—at least if they believe half we tell them,—and for delicate beauty, that rare plant, I should look among the girls of the New England hills as confidently as anywhere, and I have traveled as far south as New Jersey, and west of the Genesee Valley. Indeed, it would be easy to show that the parents of the pretty girls in the West emigrated from New England. And yet—such is the mystery of Providence—no one would expect that one of the sweetest and most delicate flowers that blooms, the trailing. arbutus, would blossom in this inhospitable climate, and peep forth from the edge of a snowbank at that.

It seems unaccountable to a superficial observer that the thousands of people who are dissatisfied with their climate do not seek a more congenial one—or stop grumbling. The world is so small, and all parts of it are so accessible, it has so many varieties of climate, that one could surely suit himself by searching; and, then, is it worth while to waste our one short life in the midst of unpleasant surroundings and in a constant friction with that which is disagreeable? One would suppose that people set down on this little globe would seek places on it most agreeable to themselves. It must be that they are much more content with the climate and country upon which they happen, by the accident of their birth, than they pretend to be.

III

Backlog Studies

Home sympathies and charities are most active in the winter. Coming in from my late walk,—in fact driven in by a hurrying north wind that would brook no delay,—a wind that brought snow that did not seem to fall out of a bounteous sky, but to be blown from polar fields,—I find the Mistress returned from town, all in a glow of philanthropic excitement.

There has been a meeting of a woman's association for Ameliorating the Condition of somebody here at home. Any one can belong to it by paying a dollar, and for twenty dollars one can become a life Ameliorator,—a sort of life assurance. The Mistress, at the meeting, I believe, "seconded the motion" several times, and is one of the Vice–Presidents; and this family honor makes me feel almost as if I were a president of something myself. These little distinctions are among the sweetest things in life, and to see one's name officially printed stimulates his charity, and is almost as satisfactory as being the chairman of a committee or the mover of a resolution. It is, I think, fortunate, and not at all discreditable, that our little vanity, which is reckoned among our weaknesses, is thus made to contribute to the activity of our nobler powers. Whatever we may say, we all of us like distinction; and probably there is no more subtle flattery than that conveyed in the whisper, "That's he," "That's she."

There used to be a society for ameliorating the condition of the Jews; but they were found to be so much more adept than other people in ameliorating their own condition that I suppose it was given up. Mandeville says that to his knowledge there are a great many people who get up ameliorating enterprises merely to be conspicuously busy in society, or to earn a little something in a good cause. They seem to think that the world owes them a living because they are philanthropists. In this Mandeville does not speak with his usual charity. It is evident that there are Jews, and some Gentiles, whose condition needs ameliorating, and if very little is really accomplished in the effort for them, it always remains true that the charitable reap a benefit to themselves. It is one of the beautiful compensations of this life that no one can sincerely try to help another without helping himself

OUR NEXT–DOOR NEIGHBOR. Why is it that almost all philanthropists and reformers are disagreeable?

I ought to explain who our next–door neighbor is. He is the person who comes in without knocking, drops in in the most natural way, as his wife does also, and not seldom in time to take the after-dinner cup of tea before the fire. Formal society begins as soon as you lock your doors, and only admit visitors through the media of bells and servants. It is lucky for us that our next-door neighbor is honest.

THE PARSON. Why do you class reformers and philanthropists together? Those usually called reformers are not philanthropists at all. They are agitators. Finding the world disagreeable to themselves, they wish to make it as unpleasant to others as possible.

MANDEVILLE. That's a noble view of your fellow-men.

OUR NEXT DOOR. Well, granting the distinction, why are both apt to be unpleasant people to live with?

THE PARSON. As if the unpleasant people who won't mind their own business were confined to the classes you mention! Some of the best people I know are philanthropists,—I mean the genuine ones, and not the uneasy busybodies seeking notoriety as a means of living.

THE FIRE-TENDER. It is not altogether the not minding their own business. Nobody does that. The usual explanation is, that people with one idea are tedious. But that is not all of it. For few persons have more than one idea,—ministers, doctors, lawyers, teachers, manufacturers, merchants,—they all think the world they live in is the central one.

MANDEVILLE. And you might add authors. To them nearly all the life of the world is in letters, and I suppose they would be astonished if they knew how little the thoughts of the majority of people are occupied with books, and with all that vast thought circulation which is the vital current of the world to book-men. Newspapers have reached their present power by becoming unliterary, and reflecting all the interests of the world.

THE MISTRESS. I have noticed one thing, that the most popular persons in society are those who take the world as it is, find the least fault, and have no hobbies. They are always wanted to dinner.

THE YOUNG LADY. And the other kind always appear to me to want a dinner.

Backlog Studies

THE FIRE–TENDER. It seems to me that the real reason why reformers and some philanthropists are unpopular is, that they disturb our serenity and make us conscious of our own shortcomings. It is only now and then that a whole people get a spasm of reformatory fervor, of investigation and regeneration. At other times they rather hate those who disturb their quiet.

OUR NEXT DOOR. Professional reformers and philanthropists are insufferably conceited and intolerant.

THE MISTRESS. Everything depends upon the spirit in which a reform or a scheme of philanthropy is conducted.

MANDEVILLE. I attended a protracted convention of reformers of a certain evil, once, and had the pleasure of taking dinner with a tableful of them. It was one of those country dinners accompanied with green tea. Every one disagreed with every one else, and you would n't wonder at it, if you had seen them. They were people with whom good food wouldn't agree. George Thompson was expected at the convention, and I remember that there was almost a cordiality in the talk about him, until one sallow brother casually mentioned that George took snuff,—when a chorus of deprecatory groans went up from the table. One long–faced maiden in spectacles, with purple ribbons in her hair, who drank five cups of tea by my count, declared that she was perfectly disgusted, and did n't want to hear him speak. In the course of the meal the talk ran upon the discipline of children, and how to administer punishment. I was quite taken by the remark of a thin, dyspeptic man who summed up the matter by growling out in a harsh, deep bass voice, "Punish 'em in love!" It sounded as if he had said, "Shoot 'em on the spot!"

THE PARSON. I supposed you would say that he was a minister. There is another thing about those people. I think they are working against the course of nature. Nature is entirely indifferent to any reform. She perpetuates a fault as persistently as a virtue. There's a split in my thumb–nail that has been scrupulously continued for many years, not withstanding all my efforts to make the nail resume its old regularity. You see the same thing in trees whose bark is cut, and in melons that have had only one summer's intimacy with squashes. The bad traits in character are passed down from generation to generation with as much care as the good ones. Nature, unaided, never reforms anything.

MANDEVILLE. Is that the essence of Calvinism?

Backlog Studies

THE PARSON. Calvinism has n't any essence, it's a fact.

MANDEVILLE. When I was a boy, I always associated Calvinism and calomel together. I thought that homeopathy—similia, etc.—had done away with both of them.

OUR NEXT DOOR (rising). If you are going into theology, I'm off..

IV

I fear we are not getting on much with the joyousness of winter. In order to be exhilarating it must be real winter. I have noticed that the lower the thermometer sinks the more fiercely the north wind rages, and the deeper the snow is, the higher rise the spirits of the community. The activity of the "elements" has a great effect upon country folk especially; and it is a more wholesome excitement than that caused by a great conflagration. The abatement of a snow–storm that grows to exceptional magnitude is regretted, for there is always the half–hope that this will be, since it has gone so far, the largest fall of snow ever known in the region, burying out of sight the great fall of 1808, the account of which is circumstantially and aggravatingly thrown in our way annually upon the least provocation. We all know how it reads: "Some said it began at daylight, others that it set in after sunrise; but all agree that by eight o'clock Friday morning it was snowing in heavy masses that darkened the air."

The morning after we settled the five—or is it seven?—points of Calvinism, there began a very hopeful snow–storm, one of those wide–sweeping, careering storms that may not much affect the city, but which strongly impress the country imagination with a sense of the personal qualities of the weather,—power, persistency, fierceness, and roaring exultation. Out–doors was terrible to those who looked out of windows, and heard the raging wind, and saw the commotion in all the high tree–tops and the writhing of the low evergreens, and could not summon resolution to go forth and breast and conquer the bluster. The sky was dark with snow, which was not permitted to fall peacefully like a blessed mantle, as it sometimes does, but was blown and rent and tossed like the split canvas of a ship in a gale. The world was taken possession of by the demons of the air, who had their will of it. There is a sort of fascination in such a scene, equal to that of a tempest at sea, and without its attendant haunting sense of peril; there is no fear that the house will founder or dash against your neighbor's cottage, which is dimly seen anchored across the field; at every thundering onset there is no fear that the cook's galley will upset, or the screw break loose and smash through the side, and we are not in momently expectation of the tinkling of the little bell to "stop her." The snow rises in drifting waves, and the naked trees bend like strained masts; but so long as the window—blinds remain fast, and the chimney—tops do not go, we preserve an equal mind. Nothing more serious can happen than the failure of the butcher's and the grocer's carts, unless, indeed, the little news—carrier should fail to board us with the world's daily bulletin, or our next—door neighbor should be deterred from coming to sit by the blazing, excited fire, and interchange the trifling, harmless gossip of the day. The feeling of seclusion on such a day is sweet, but the true friend who does brave the storm and come is welcomed with a sort of enthusiasm that his arrival in pleasant weather would never excite. The snow—bound in their Arctic hulk are glad to see even a wandering Esquimau.

On such a day I recall the great snow—storms on the northern New England hills, which lasted for a week with no cessation, with no sunrise or sunset, and no observation at noon; and the sky all the while dark with the driving snow, and the whole world full of the noise of the rioting Boreal forces; until the roads were obliterated, the fences covered, and the snow was piled solidly above the first— story windows of the farmhouse on one side, and drifted before the front door so high that egress could only be had by tunneling the bank.

After such a battle and siege, when the wind fell and the sun struggled out again, the pallid world lay subdued and tranquil, and the scattered dwellings were not unlike wrecks stranded by the tempest and half buried in sand. But when the blue sky again bent over all, the wide expanse of snow sparkled like diamond—fields, and the chimney signal—smokes could be seen, how beautiful was the picture! Then began the stir abroad, and the efforts to open up communication through roads, or fields, or wherever paths could be broken, and the ways to the meeting—house first of all. Then from every house and hamlet the men turned out with shovels, with the patient, lumbering oxen yoked to the sleds, to break the roads, driving into the deepest drifts, shoveling and shouting as if the severe labor were a holiday frolic, the courage and the hilarity rising with the difficulties encountered; and relief parties, meeting at length in the midst of the wide white desolation, hailed each other as chance explorers in new lands, and made the whole country—side ring with the noise of their congratulations. There was as much excitement and healthy stirring of the blood in it as in the Fourth of July, and perhaps as much patriotism. The boy saw it in dumb show from the distant, low farmhouse window, and wished he were a man. At night there were great stories of achievement told by the cavernous fireplace; great latitude was permitted in the estimation of the size of particular drifts, but never any agreement was reached as to the "depth on a level." I have observed since that people are quite as apt to agree upon the marvelous and the exceptional as upon simple facts.

V

By the firelight and the twilight, the Young Lady is finishing a letter to Herbert,—writing it, literally, on her knees, transforming thus the simple deed into an act of devotion. Mandeville says that it is bad for her eyes, but the sight of it is worse for his eyes. He begins to doubt the wisdom of reliance upon that worn apothegm about absence conquering love.

Memory has the singular characteristic of recalling in a friend absent, as in a journey long past, only that which is agreeable. Mandeville begins to wish he were in New South Wales.

I did intend to insert here a letter of Herbert's to the Young Lady, —obtained, I need not say, honorably, as private letters which get into print always are,—not to gratify a vulgar curiosity, but

to show how the most unsentimental and cynical people are affected by the master passion. But I cannot bring myself to do it. Even in the interests of science one has no right to make an autopsy of two loving hearts, especially when they are suffering under a late attack of the one agreeable epidemic.

All the world loves a lover, but it laughs at him none the less in his extravagances. He loses his accustomed reticence; he has something of the martyr's willingness for publicity; he would even like to show the sincerity of his devotion by some piece of open heroism. Why should he conceal a discovery which has transformed the world to him, a secret which explains all the mysteries of nature and human–ity? He is in that ecstasy of mind which prompts those who were never orators before to rise in an experience–meeting and pour out a flood of feeling in the tritest language and the most conventional terms. I am not sure that Herbert, while in this glow, would be ashamed of his letter in print, but this is one of the cases where chancery would step in and protect one from himself by his next friend. This is really a delicate matter, and perhaps it is brutal to allude to it at all.

In truth, the letter would hardly be interesting in print. Love has a marvelous power of vivifying language and charging the simplest words with the most tender meaning, of restoring to them the power they had when first coined. They are words of fire to those two who know their secret, but not to others. It is generally admitted that the best love–letters would not make very good literature. "Dearest," begins Herbert, in a burst of originality, felicitously selecting a word whose exclusiveness shuts out all the world but one, and which is a whole letter, poem, confession, and creed in one breath. What a weight of meaning it has to carry! There may be beauty and wit and grace and naturalness and even the splendor of fortune elsewhere, but there is one woman in the world whose sweet presence would be compensation for the loss of all else. It is not to be reasoned about; he wants that one; it is her plume dancing down the sunny street that sets his heart beating; he knows her form among a thousand, and follows her; he longs to run after her carriage, which the cruel coachman whirls out of his sight. It is marvelous to him that all the world does not want her too, and he is in a panic when he thinks of it. And what exquisite flattery is in that little word addressed to her, and with what sweet and meek triumph she repeats it to herself, with a feeling that is not altogether pity for those who still stand and wait. To be chosen out of all the available world—it is almost as much bliss as it is to choose. "All that long, long stage–ride from Blim's to Portage I thought of you every moment, and wondered what you were doing and how you were looking just that moment, and I found the occupation so charming that I was almost sorry when the journey was ended." Not much in that! But I have no doubt the Young Lady read it over and over, and dwelt also upon every moment, and found in it new proof of unshaken constancy, and had in that and the like things in the letter a sense of the sweetest communion. There is nothing in this letter that we need dwell on it, but I am convinced that the mail does not carry any other letters so valuable as this sort.

I suppose that the appearance of Herbert in this new light unconsciously gave tone a little to the evening's talk; not that anybody mentioned him, but Mandeville was evidently generalizing from the qualities that make one person admired by another to those that win the love of mankind.

MANDEVILLE. There seems to be something in some persons that wins them liking, special or general, independent almost of what they do or say.

THE MISTRESS. Why, everybody is liked by some one.

MANDEVILLE. I'm not sure of that. There are those who are friendless, and would be if they had endless acquaintances. But, to take the case away from ordinary examples, in which habit and a thousand circumstances influence liking, what is it that determines the world upon a personal regard for authors whom it has never seen?

THE FIRE–TENDER. Probably it is the spirit shown in their writings.

THE MISTRESS. More likely it is a sort of tradition; I don't believe that the world has a feeling of personal regard for any author who was not loved by those who knew him most intimately.

THE FIRE–TENDFR. Which comes to the same thing. The qualities, the spirit, that got him the love of his acquaintances he put into his books.

MANDEVILLE. That does n't seem to me sufficient. Shakespeare has put everything into his plays and poems, swept the whole range of human sympathies and passions, and at times is inspired by the sweetest spirit that ever man had.

THE YOUNG LADY. No one has better interpreted love.

MANDEVILLE. Yet I apprehend that no person living has any personal regard for Shakespeare, or that his personality affects many,—except they stand in Stratford church and feel a sort of awe at the thought that the bones of the greatest poet are so near them.

THE PARSON. I don't think the world cares personally for any mere man or woman dead for centuries.

MANDEVILLE. But there is a difference. I think there is still rather a warm feeling for Socrates the man, independent of what he said, which is little known. Homer's works are certainly better known, but no one cares personally for Homer any more than for any other shade.

OUR NEXT DOOR. Why not go back to Moses? We've got the evening before us for digging up people.

MANDEVILLE. Moses is a very good illustration. No name of antiquity is better known, and yet I fancy he does not awaken the same kind of popular liking that Socrates does.

OUR NEXT DOOR. Fudge! You just get up in any lecture assembly and propose three cheers for Socrates, and see where you'll be. Mandeville ought to be a missionary, and read Robert Browning to the Fijis.

THE FIRE—TENDER. How do you account for the alleged personal regard for Socrates?

THE PARSON. Because the world called Christian is still more than half heathen.

MANDEVILLE. He was a plain man; his sympathies were with the people; he had what is roughly known as "horse—sense," and he was homely. Franklin and Abraham Lincoln belong to his class. They were all philosophers of the shrewd sort, and they all had humor. It was fortunate for Lincoln that, with his other qualities, he was homely. That was the last touching recommendation to the popular heart.

THE MISTRESS. Do you remember that ugly brown—stone statue of St. Antonio by the bridge in Sorrento? He must have been a coarse saint, patron of pigs as he was, but I don't know any one anywhere, or the homely stone image of one, so loved by the people.

OUR NEXT DOOR. Ugliness being trump, I wonder more people don't win. Mandeville, why don't you get up a "centenary" of Socrates, and put up his statue in the Central Park? It would make that one of Lincoln in Union Square look beautiful.

THE PARSON. Oh, you'll see that some day, when they have a museum there illustrating the "Science of Religion."

THE FIRE—TENDER. Doubtless, to go back to what we were talking of, the world has a fondness for some authors, and thinks of them with an affectionate and half—pitying familiarity; and it may be that this grows out of something in their lives quite as much as anything in their writings. There seems to be more disposition of personal liking to Thackeray than to Dickens, now both are dead,—a result that would hardly have been predicted when the world was crying over Little Nell, or agreeing to hate Becky Sharp.

THE YOUNG LADY. What was that you were telling about Charles Lamb, the other day, Mandeville? Is not the popular liking for him somewhat independent of his writings?

MANDEVILLE. He is a striking example of an author who is loved. Very likely the remembrance of his tribulations has still something to do with the tenderness felt for him. He supported no dignity and permitted a familiarity which indicated no self−appreciation of his real rank in the world of letters. I have heard that his acquaintances familiarly called him "Charley."

OUR NEXT DOOR. It's a relief to know that! Do you happen to know what Socrates was called?

MANDEVILLE. I have seen people who knew Lamb very well. One of them told me, as illustrating his want of dignity, that as he was going home late one night through the nearly empty streets, he was met by a roystering party who were making a night of it from tavern to tavern. They fell upon Lamb, attracted by his odd figure and hesitating manner, and, hoisting him on their shoulders, carried him off, singing as they went. Lamb enjoyed the lark, and did not tell them who he was. When they were tired of lugging him, they lifted him, with much effort and difficulty, to the top of a high wall, and left him there amid the broken bottles, utterly unable to get down. Lamb remained there philosophically in the enjoyment of his novel adventure, until a passing watchman rescued him from his ridiculous situation.

THE FIRE−TENDER. How did the story get out?

MANDEVILLE. Oh, Lamb told all about it next morning; and when asked afterwards why he did so, he replied that there was no fun in it unless he told it.

SIXTH STUDY

I

The King sat in the winter−house in the ninth month, and there was a fire on the hearth burning before him . . . . When Jehudi had read three or four leaves he cut it with the penknife.

Backlog Studies

That seems to be a pleasant and home–like picture from a not very remote period,—less than twenty–five hundred years ago, and many centuries after the fall of Troy. And that was not so very long ago, for Thebes, in the splendid streets of which Homer wandered and sang to the kings when Memphis, whose ruins are older than history, was its younger rival, was twelve centuries old when Paris ran away with Helen.

I am sorry that the original—and you can usually do anything with the "original"—does not bear me out in saying that it was a pleasant picture. I should like to believe that Jehoiakiin—for that was the singular name of the gentleman who sat by his hearthstone—had just received the Memphis "Palimpsest," fifteen days in advance of the date of its publication, and that his secretary was reading to him that monthly, and cutting its leaves as he read. I should like to have seen it in that year when Thales was learning astronomy in Memphis, and Necho was organizing his campaign against Carchemish. If Jehoiakim took the "Attic Quarterly," he might have read its comments on the banishment of the Alcmaeonida:, and its gibes at Solon for his prohibitory laws, forbidding the sale of unguents, limiting the luxury of dress, and interfering with the sacred rights of mourners to passionately bewail the dead in the Asiatic manner; the same number being enriched with contributions from two rising poets,—a lyric of love by Sappho, and an ode sent by Anacreon from Teos, with an editorial note explaining that the Maces was not responsible for the sentiments of the poem.

But, in fact, the gentleman who sat before the backlog in his winter–house had other things to think of. For Nebuchadnezzar was coming that way with the chariots and horses of Babylon and a great crowd of marauders; and the king had not even the poor choice whether he would be the vassal of the Chaldean or of the Egyptian. To us, this is only a ghostly show of monarchs and conquerors stalking across vast historic spaces. It was no doubt a vulgar enough scene of war and plunder. The great captains of that age went about to harry each other's territories and spoil each other's cities very much as we do nowadays, and for similar reasons;—Napoleon the Great in Moscow, Napoleon the Small in Italy, Kaiser William in Paris, Great Scott in Mexico! Men have not changed much.

—The Fire–Tender sat in his winter–garden in the third month; there was a fire on the hearth burning before him. He cut the leaves of "Scribner's Monthly" with his penknife, and thought of Jehoiakim.

Backlog Studies

That seems as real as the other. In the garden, which is a room of the house, the tall callas, rooted in the ground, stand about the fountain; the sun, streaming through the glass, illumines the many–hued flowers. I wonder what Jehoiakim did with the mealy–bug on his passion–vine, and if he had any way of removing the scale–bug from his African acacia? One would like to know, too, how he treated the red spider on the Le Marque rose. The record is silent. I do not doubt he had all these insects in his winter–garden, and the aphidae besides; and he could not smoke them out with tobacco, for the world had not yet fallen into its second stage of the knowledge of good and evil by eating the forbidden tobacco–plant.

I confess that this little picture of a fire on the hearth so many centuries ago helps to make real and interesting to me that somewhat misty past. No doubt the lotus and the acanthus from the Nile grew in that winter–house, and perhaps Jehoiakim attempted—the most difficult thing in the world the cultivation of the wild flowers from Lebanon. Perhaps Jehoiakim was interested also, as I am through this ancient fireplace,—which is a sort of domestic window into the ancient world,—in the loves of Bernice and Abaces at the court of the Pharaohs. I see that it is the same thing as the sentiment— perhaps it is the shrinking which every soul that is a soul has, sooner or later, from isolation—which grew up between Herbert and the Young Lady Staying With Us. Jeremiah used to come in to that fireside very much as the Parson does to ours. The Parson, to be sure, never prophesies, but he grumbles, and is the chorus in the play that sings the everlasting ai ai of "I told you so!" Yet we like the Parson. He is the sprig of bitter herb that makes the pottage wholesome. I should rather, ten times over, dispense with the flatterers and the smooth–sayers than the grumblers. But the grumblers are of two sorts,—the healthful–toned and the whiners. There are makers of beer who substitute for the clean bitter of the hops some deleterious drug, and then seek to hide the fraud by some cloying sweet. There is nothing of this sickish drug in the Parson's talk, nor was there in that of Jeremiah, I sometimes think there is scarcely enough of this wholesome tonic in modern society. The Parson says he never would give a child sugar–coated pills. Mandeville says he never would give them any. After all, you cannot help liking Mandeville.

II

We were talking of this late news from Jerusalem. The Fire–Tender was saying that it is astonishing how much is telegraphed us from the East that is not half so interesting. He was at a loss philosophically to account for the fact that the world is so eager to know the news of yesterday which is unimportant, and so indifferent to that of the day before which is of some moment.

MANDEVILLE. I suspect that it arises from the want of imagination. People need to touch the facts, and nearness in time is contiguity. It would excite no interest to bulletin the last siege of Jerusalem in a village where the event was unknown, if the date was appended; and yet the account of it is incomparably more exciting than that of the siege of Metz.

OUR NEXT DOOR. The daily news is a necessity. I cannot get along without my morning paper. The other morning I took it up, and was absorbed in the telegraphic columns for an hour nearly. I thoroughly enjoyed the feeling of immediate contact with all the world of yesterday, until I read among the minor items that Patrick Donahue, of the city of New York, died of a sunstroke. If he had frozen to death, I should have enjoyed that; but to die of sunstroke in February seemed inappropriate, and I turned to the date of the paper. When I found it was printed in July, I need not say that I lost all interest in it, though why the trivialities and crimes and accidents, relating to people I never knew, were not as good six months after date as twelve hours, I cannot say.

THE FIRE–TENDER. You know that in Concord the latest news, except a remark or two by Thoreau or Emerson, is the Vedas. I believe the Rig–Veda is read at the breakfast–table instead of the Boston journals.

THE PARSON. I know it is read afterward instead of the Bible.

MANDEVILLE. That is only because it is supposed to be older. I have understood that the Bible is very well spoken of there, but it is not antiquated enough to be an authority.

OUR NEXT DOOR. There was a project on foot to put it into the circulating library, but the title New in the second part was considered objectionable.

HERBERT. Well, I have a good deal of sympathy with Concord as to the news. We are fed on a daily diet of trivial events and gossip, of the unfruitful sayings of thoughtless men and women, until our mental digestion is seriously impaired; the day will come when no one will be able to sit down to a thoughtful, well–wrought book and assimilate its contents.

THE MISTRESS. I doubt if a daily newspaper is a necessity, in the higher sense of the word.

THE PARSON. Nobody supposes it is to women,—that is, if they can see each other.

THE MISTRESS. Don't interrupt, unless you have something to say; though I should like to know how much gossip there is afloat that the minister does not know. The newspaper may be needed in society, but how quickly it drops out of mind when one goes beyond the bounds of what is called civilization. You remember when we were in the depths of the woods last summer how difficult it was to get up any interest in the files of late papers that reached us, and how unreal all the struggle and turmoil of the world seemed. We stood apart, and could estimate things at their true value.

THE YOUNG LADY. Yes, that was real life. I never tired of the guide's stories; there was some interest in the intelligence that a deer had been down to eat the lily–pads at the foot of the lake the night before; that a bear's track was seen on the trail we crossed that day; even Mandeville's fish–stories had a certain air of probability; and how to roast a trout in the ashes and serve him hot and juicy and clean, and how to cook soup and prepare coffee and heat dish–water in one tin–pail, were vital problems.

THE PARSON. You would have had no such problems at home. Why will people go so far to put themselves to such inconvenience? I hate the woods. Isolation breeds conceit; there are no people so conceited as those who dwell in remote wildernesses and live mostly alone.

THE YOUNG LADY. For my part, I feel humble in the presence of mountains, and in the vast stretches of the wilderness.

THE PARSON. I'll be bound a woman would feel just as nobody would expect her to feel, under given circumstances.

MANDEVILLE. I think the reason why the newspaper and the world it carries take no hold of us in the wilderness is that we become a kind of vegetable ourselves when we go there. I have often attempted to improve my mind in the woods with good solid books. You might as well offer a bunch of celery to an oyster. The mind goes to sleep: the senses and the instincts wake up. The best I can do when it rains, or the trout won't bite, is to read Dumas's novels. Their ingenuity will almost keep a man awake after supper, by the camp–fire. And there is a kind of unity about them that I like; the history is as good as the morality.

OUR NEXT DOOR. I always wondered where Mandeville got his historical facts.

THE MISTRESS. Mandeville misrepresents himself in the woods. I heard him one night repeat "The Vision of Sir Launfal"—(THE FIRE–TENDER. Which comes very near being our best poem.)—as we were crossing the lake, and the guides became so absorbed in it that they forgot to paddle, and sat listening with open mouths, as if it had been a panther story.

THE PARSON. Mandeville likes to show off well enough. I heard that he related to a woods' boy up there the whole of the Siege of Troy. The boy was very much interested, and said "there'd been a man up there that spring from Troy, looking up timber." Mandeville always carries the news when he goes into the country.

MANDEVILLE. I'm going to take the Parson's sermon on Jonah next summer; it's the nearest to anything like news we've had from his pulpit in ten years. But, seriously, the boy was very well informed. He'd heard of Albany; his father took in the "Weekly Tribune," and he had a partial conception of Horace Greeley.

OUR NEXT DOOR. I never went so far out of the world in America yet that the name of Horace Greeley did n't rise up before me. One of the first questions asked by any camp–fire is, "Did ye ever see Horace?"

HERBERT. Which shows the power of the press again. But I have often remarked how little real conception of the moving world, as it is, people in remote regions get from the newspaper. It needs to be read in the midst of events. A chip cast ashore in a refluent eddy tells no tale of the force and swiftness of the current.

OUR NEXT DOOR. I don't exactly get the drift of that last remark; but I rather like a remark that I can't understand; like the landlady's indigestible bread, it stays by you.

HERBERT. I see that I must talk in words of one syllable. The newspaper has little effect upon the remote country mind, because the remote country mind is interested in a very limited number of things. Besides, as the Parson says, it is conceited. The most accomplished scholar will be the butt of all the guides in the woods, because he cannot follow a trail that would puzzle a sable (saple the trappers call it).

THE PARSON. It's enough to read the summer letters that people write to the newspapers from the country and the woods. Isolated from the activity of the world, they come to think that the little adventures of their stupid days and nights are important. Talk about that being real life! Compare the letters such people write with the other contents of the newspaper, and you will see which life is real. That's one reason I hate to have summer come, the country letters set in.

THE MISTRESS. I should like to see something the Parson does n't hate to have come.

MANDEVILLE. Except his quarter's salary; and the meeting of the American Board.

THE FIRE–TENDER. I don't see that we are getting any nearer the solution of the original question. The world is evidently interested in events simply because they are recent.

OUR NEXT DOOR. I have a theory that a newspaper might be published at little cost, merely by reprinting the numbers of years before, only altering the dates; just as the Parson preaches over his sermons.

THE FIRE–TENDER. It's evident we must have a higher order of news–gatherers. It has come to this, that the newspaper furnishes thought–material for all the world, actually prescribes from day to day the themes the world shall think on and talk about. The occupation of news–gathering becomes, therefore, the most important. When you think of it, it is astonishing that this department should not be in the hands of the ablest men, accomplished scholars, philosophical observers, discriminating selectors of the news of the world that is worth thinking over and talking about. The editorial comments frequently are able enough, but is it worth while keeping an expensive mill going to grind chaff? I sometimes wonder, as I open my morning paper, if nothing did happen in the twenty–four hours except crimes, accidents, defalcations, deaths of unknown loafers, robberies, monstrous births,—say about the level of police–court news.

Backlog Studies

OUR NEXT DOOR. I have even noticed that murders have deteriorated; they are not so high-toned and mysterious as they used to be.

THE FIRE-TENDER. It is true that the newspapers have improved vastly within the last decade.

HERBERT. I think, for one, that they are very much above the level of the ordinary gossip of the country.

THE FIRE-TENDER. But I am tired of having the under-world still occupy so much room in the newspapers. The reporters are rather more alert for a dog-fight than a philological convention. It must be that the good deeds of the world outnumber the bad in any given day; and what a good reflex action it would have on society if they could be more fully reported than the bad! I suppose the Parson would call this the Enthusiasm of Humanity.

THE PARSON. You'll see how far you can lift yourself up by your boot-straps.

HERBERT. I wonder what influence on the quality (I say nothing of quantity) of news the coming of women into the reporter's and editor's work will have.

OUR NEXT DOOR. There are the baby-shows; they make cheerful reading.

THE MISTRESS. All of them got up by speculating men, who impose upon the vanity of weak women.

HERBERT. I think women reporters are more given to personal details and gossip than the men. When I read the Washington correspondence I am proud of my country, to see how many Apollo Belvederes, Adonises, how much marble brow and piercing eye and hyacinthine locks, we have in the two houses of Congress.

THE YOUNG LADY. That's simply because women understand the personal weakness of men; they have a long score of personal flattery to pay off too.

MANDEVILLE. I think women will bring in elements of brightness, picturesqueness, and purity very much needed. Women have a power of investing simple ordinary things with a charm; men are bungling narrators compared with them.

THE PARSON. The mistake they make is in trying to write, and especially to "stump—speak," like men; next to an effeminate man there is nothing so disagreeable as a mannish woman.

HERBERT. I heard one once address a legislative committee. The knowing air, the familiar, jocular, smart manner, the nodding and winking innuendoes, supposed to be those of a man "up to snuff," and au fait in political wiles, were inexpressibly comical. And yet the exhibition was pathetic, for it had the suggestive vulgarity of a woman in man's clothes. The imitation is always a dreary failure.

THE MISTRESS. Such women are the rare exceptions. I am ready to defend my sex; but I won't attempt to defend both sexes in one.

THE FIRE—TENDER. I have great hope that women will bring into the newspaper an elevating influence; the common and sweet life of society is much better fitted to entertain and instruct us than the exceptional and extravagant. I confess (saving the Mistress's presence) that the evening talk over the dessert at dinner is much more entertaining and piquant than the morning paper, and often as important.

THE MISTRESS. I think the subject had better be changed.

MANDEVILLE. The person, not the subject. There is no entertainment so full of quiet pleasure as the hearing a lady of cultivation and refinement relate her day's experience in her daily rounds of calls, charitable visits, shopping, errands of relief and condolence. The evening budget is better than the finance minister's.

OUR NEXT DOOR. That's even so. My wife will pick up more news in six hours than I can get in a week, and I'm fond of news.

MANDEVILLE. I don't mean gossip, by any means, or scandal. A woman of culture skims over that like a bird, never touching it with the tip of a wing. What she brings home is the freshness and brightness of life. She touches everything so daintily, she hits off a character in a sentence, she gives the pith of a dialogue without tediousness, she mimics without vulgarity; her narration sparkles, but it does n't sting. The picture of her day is full of vivacity, and it gives new value and freshness to common things. If we could only have on the stage such actresses as we have in the drawing–room!

THE FIRE–TENDER. We want something more of this grace, sprightliness, and harmless play of the finer life of society in the newspaper.

OUR NEXT DOOR. I wonder Mandeville does n't marry, and become a permanent subscriber to his embodied idea of a newspaper.

THE YOUNG LADY. Perhaps he does not relish the idea of being unable to stop his subscription.

OUR NEXT DOOR. Parson, won't you please punch that fire, and give us more blaze? we are getting into the darkness of socialism.

III

Herbert returned to us in March. The Young Lady was spending the winter with us, and March, in spite of the calendar, turned out to be a winter month. It usually is in New England, and April too, for that matter. And I cannot say it is unfortunate for us. There are so many topics to be turned over and settled at our fireside that a winter of ordinary length would make little impression on the list. The fireside is, after all, a sort of private court of chancery, where nothing ever does come to a final decision. The chief effect of talk on any subject is to strengthen one's own opinions, and, in fact, one never knows exactly what he does believe until he is warmed into conviction by the heat of attack and defence. A man left to himself drifts about like a boat on a calm lake; it is only when the wind blows that the boat goes anywhere.

Herbert said he had been dipping into the recent novels written by women, here and there, with a view to noting the effect upon literature of this sudden and rather overwhelming accession to it. There was a good deal of talk about it evening after evening, off and on, and I can only undertake to set down fragments of it.

HERBERT. I should say that the distinguishing feature of the literature of this day is the prominence women have in its production. They figure in most of the magazines, though very rarely in the scholarly and critical reviews, and in thousands of newspapers; to them we are indebted for the oceans of Sunday–school books, and they write the majority of the novels, the serial stories, and they mainly pour out the watery flood of tales in the weekly papers. Whether this is to result in more good than evil it is impossible yet to say, and perhaps it would be unjust to say, until this generation has worked off its froth, and women settle down to artistic, conscien–tious labor in literature.

THE MISTRESS. You don't mean to say that George Eliot, and Mrs. Gaskell, and George Sand, and Mrs. Browning, before her marriage and severe attack of spiritism, are less true to art than contemporary men novelists and poets.

HERBERT. You name some exceptions that show the bright side of the picture, not only for the present, but for the future. Perhaps genius has no sex; but ordinary talent has. I refer to the great body of novels, which you would know by internal evidence were written by women. They are of two sorts: the domestic story, entirely unidealized, and as flavorless as water–gruel; and the spiced novel, generally immoral in tendency, in which the social problems are handled, unhappy marriages, affinity and passional attraction, bigamy, and the violation of the seventh commandment. These subjects are treated in the rawest manner, without any settled ethics, with little discrimination of eternal right and wrong, and with very little sense of responsibility for what is set forth. Many of these novels are merely the blind outbursts of a nature impatient of restraint and the conventionalities of society, and are as chaotic as the untrained minds that produce them.

MANDEVILLE. Don't you think these novels fairly represent a social condition of unrest and upheaval?

HERBERT. Very likely; and they help to create and spread abroad the discontent they describe. Stories of bigamy (sometimes disguised by divorce), of unhappy marriages, where the injured wife, through an entire volume, is on the brink of falling into the arms of a sneaking lover, until death kindly removes the obstacle, and the two souls, who were born for each other, but got separated in the cradle, melt and mingle into one in the last chapter, are not healthful reading for maids or mothers.

THE MISTRESS. Or men.

THE FIRE–TENDER. The most disagreeable object to me in modern literature is the man the women novelists have introduced as the leading character; the women who come in contact with him seem to be fascinated by his disdainful mien, his giant strength, and his brutal manner. He is broad across the shoulders, heavily moulded, yet as lithe as a cat; has an ugly scar across his right cheek; has been in the four quarters of the globe; knows seventeen languages; had a harem in Turkey and a Fayaway in the Marquesas; can be as polished as Bayard in the drawing–room, but is as gloomy as Conrad in the library; has a terrible eye and a withering glance, but can be instantly subdued by a woman's hand, if it is not his wife's; and through all his morose and vicious career has carried a heart as pure as a violet.

THE MISTRESS. Don't you think the Count of Monte Cristo is the elder brother of Rochester?

THE FIRE–TENDER. One is a mere hero of romance; the other is meant for a real man.

MANDEVILLE. I don't see that the men novel–writers are better than the women.

HERBERT. That's not the question; but what are women who write so large a proportion of the current stories bringing into literature? Aside from the question of morals, and the absolutely demoralizing manner of treating social questions, most of their stories are vapid and weak beyond expression, and are slovenly in composition, showing neither study, training, nor mental discipline.

THE MISTRESS. Considering that women have been shut out from the training of the universities, and have few opportunities for the wide observation that men enjoy, isn't it pretty well that the foremost living writers of fiction are women?

HERBERT. You can say that for the moment, since Thackeray and Dickens have just died. But it does not affect the general estimate. We are inundated with a flood of weak writing. Take the Sunday– school literature, largely the product of women; it has n't as much character as a dried apple pie. I don't know what we are coming to if the presses keep on running.

OUR NEXT DOOR. We are living, we are dwelling, in a grand and awful time; I'm glad I don't write novels.

THE PARSON. So am I.

OUR NEXT DOOR. I tried a Sunday—school book once; but I made the good boy end in the poorhouse, and the bad boy go to Congress; and the publisher said it wouldn't do, the public wouldn't stand that sort of thing. Nobody but the good go to Congress.

THE MISTRESS. Herbert, what do you think women are good for?

OUR NEXT DOOR. That's a poser.

HERBERT. Well, I think they are in a tentative state as to literature, and we cannot yet tell what they will do. Some of our most brilliant books of travel, correspondence, and writing on topics in which their sympathies have warmly interested them, are by women. Some of them are also strong writers in the daily journals.

MANDEVILLE. I 'm not sure there's anything a woman cannot do as well as a man, if she sets her heart on it.

THE PARSON. That's because she's no conscience.

CHORUS. O Parson!

THE PARSON. Well, it does n't trouble her, if she wants to do anything. She looks at the end, not the means. A woman, set on anything, will walk right through the moral crockery without wincing. She'd be a great deal more unscrupulous in politics than the average man. Did you ever see a female lobbyist? Or a criminal? It is Lady Macbeth who does not falter. Don't raise your hands at me! The sweetest angel or the coolest devil is a woman. I see in some of the modern novels we have been talking of the same unscrupulous daring, a blindness to moral distinctions, a constant exaltation of a passion into a virtue, an entire disregard of the immutable laws on which the family and society rest. And you ask lawyers and trustees how scrupulous women are in business transactions!

THE FIRE—TENDER. Women are often ignorant of affairs, and, besides, they may have a notion often that a woman ought to be privileged more than a man in business matters; but I tell you, as a rule, that if men would consult their wives, they would go a deal straighter in business operations than they do go.

THE PARSON. We are all poor sinners. But I've another indictment against the women writers. We get no good old–fashioned love–stories from them. It's either a quarrel of discordant natures one a panther, and the other a polar bear—for courtship, until one of them is crippled by a railway accident; or a long wrangle of married life between two unpleasant people, who can neither live comfortably together nor apart. I suppose, by what I see, that sweet wooing, with all its torturing and delightful uncertainty, still goes on in the world; and I have no doubt that the majority of married people live more happily than the unmarried. But it's easier to find a dodo than a new and good love–story.

MANDEVILLE. I suppose the old style of plot is exhausted. Everything in man and outside of him has been turned over so often that I should think the novelists would cease simply from want of material.

THE PARSON. Plots are no more exhausted than men are. Every man is a new creation, and combinations are simply endless. Even if we did not have new material in the daily change of society, and there were only a fixed number of incidents and characters in life, invention could not be exhausted on them. I amuse myself sometimes with my kaleidoscope, but I can never reproduce a figure. No, no. I cannot say that you may not exhaust everything else: we may get all the secrets of a nature into a book by and by, but the novel is immortal, for it deals with men.

The Parson's vehemence came very near carrying him into a sermon; and as nobody has the privilege of replying to his sermons, so none of the circle made any reply now.

Our Next Door mumbled something about his hair standing on end, to hear a minister defending the novel; but it did not interrupt the general silence. Silence is unnoticed when people sit before a fire; it would be intolerable if they sat and looked at each other.

The wind had risen during the evening, and Mandeville remarked, as they rose to go, that it had a spring sound in it, but it was as cold as winter. The Mistress said she heard a bird that morning singing in the sun a spring song, it was a winter bird, but it sang

SEVENTH STUDY

We have been much interested in what is called the Gothic revival. We have spent I don't know how many evenings in looking over Herbert's plans for a cottage, and have been amused with his vain efforts to cover with Gothic roofs the vast number of large rooms which the Young Lady draws in her sketch of a small house.

I have no doubt that the Gothic, which is capable of infinite modification, so that every house built in that style may be as different from every other house as one tree is from every other, can be adapted to our modern uses, and will be, when artists catch its spirit instead of merely copying its old forms. But just now we are taking the Gothic very literally, as we took the Greek at one time, or as we should probably have taken the Saracenic, if the Moors had not been colored. Not even the cholera is so contagious in this country as a style of architecture which we happen to catch; the country is just now broken out all over with the Mansard—roof epidemic.

And in secular architecture we do not study what is adapted to our climate any more than in ecclesiastic architecture we adopt that which is suited to our religion.

We are building a great many costly churches here and there, we Protestants, and as the most of them are ill adapted to our forms of worship, it may be necessary and best for us to change our religion in order to save our investments. I am aware that this would be a grave step, and we should not hasten to throw overboard Luther and the right of private judgment without reflection. And yet, if it is necessary to revive the ecclesiastical Gothic architecture, not in its spirit (that we nowhere do), but in the form which served another age and another faith, and if, as it appears, we have already a great deal of money invested in this reproduction, it may be more prudent to go forward than to go back. The question is, "Cannot one easier change his creed than his pew?"

I occupy a seat in church which is an admirable one for reflection, but I cannot see or hear much that is going on in what we like to call the apse. There is a splendid stone pillar, a clustered column, right in front of me, and I am as much protected from the minister as Old Put's troops were from the British, behind the stone wall at Bunker's Hill. I can hear his voice occasionally wandering round in the arches overhead, and I recognize the tone, because he is a friend of mine and an excellent man, but what he is saying I can very seldom make out. If there was any incense burning, I could smell it, and that would be something. I rather like the smell of incense, and it has its holy associations. But there is no smell in our church, except of bad air,—for there is no provision for ventilation in the splendid and costly edifice. The reproduction of the old Gothic is so complete that the builders even seem to have brought over the ancient air from one of the churches of the Middle Ages,—you would declare it had n't been changed in two centuries.

I am expected to fix my attention during the service upon one man, who stands in the centre of the apse and has a sounding–board behind him in order to throw his voice out of the sacred semicircular space (where the aitar used to stand, but now the sounding–board takes the place of the altar) and scatter it over the congregation at large, and send it echoing up in the groined roof I always like to hear a minister who is unfamiliar with the house, and who has a loud voice, try to fill the edifice. The more he roars and gives himself with vehemence to the effort, the more the building roars in indistinguishable noise and hubbub. By the time he has said (to suppose a case), "The Lord is in his holy temple," and has passed on to say, "let all the earth keep silence," the building is repeating "The Lord is in his holy temple" from half a dozen different angles and altitudes, rolling it and growling it, and is not keeping silence at all. A man who understands it waits until the house has had its say, and has digested one passage, before he launches another into the vast, echoing spaces. I am expected, as I said, to fix my eye and mind on the minister, the central point of the service. But the pillar hides him. Now if there were several ministers in the church, dressed in such gorgeous colors that I could see them at the distance from the apse at which my limited income compels me to sit, and candles were burning, and censers were swinging, and the platform was full of the sacred bustle of a gorgeous ritual worship, and a bell rang to tell me the holy moments, I should not mind the pillar at all. I should sit there, like any other Goth, and enjoy it. But, as I have said, the pastor is a friend of mine, and I like to look at him on Sunday, and hear what he says, for he always says something worth hearing. I am on such terms with him, indeed we all are, that it would be pleasant to have the service of a little more social nature, and more human. When we put him away off in the apse, and set him up for a Goth, and then seat ourselves at a distance, scattered about among the pillars, the whole thing seems to me a trifle unnatural. Though I do not mean to say that the congregations do not "enjoy their religion " in their splendid edifices which cost so much money and are really so beautiful.

A good many people have the idea, so it seems, that Gothic architecture and Christianity are essentially one and the same thing. Just as many regard it as an act of piety to work an altar cloth or to cushion a pulpit. It may be, and it may not be.

Backlog Studies

Our Gothic church is likely to prove to us a valuable religious experience, bringing out many of the Christian virtues. It may have had its origin in pride, but it is all being overruled for our good. Of course I need n't explain that it is the thirteenth century ecclesiastic Gothic that is epidemic in this country; and I think it has attacked the Congregational and the other non–ritual churches more violently than any others. We have had it here in its most beautiful and dangerous forms. I believe we are pretty much all of us supplied with a Gothic church now. Such has been the enthusiasm in this devout direction, that I should not be surprised to see our rich private citizens putting up Gothic churches for their individual amusement and sanctification. As the day will probably come when every man in Hartford will live in his own mammoth, five–story granite insurance building, it may not be unreasonable to expect that every man will sport his own Gothic church. It is beginning to be discovered that the Gothic sort of church edifice is fatal to the Congregational style of worship that has been prevalent here in New England; but it will do nicely (as they say in Boston) for private devotion.

There isn't a finer or purer church than ours any where, inside and outside Gothic to the last. The elevation of the nave gives it even that "high–shouldered" appearance which seemed more than anything else to impress Mr. Hawthorne in the cathedral at Amiens. I fancy that for genuine high–shoulderness we are not exceeded by any church in the city. Our chapel in the rear is as Gothic as the rest of it,– –a beautiful little edifice. The committee forgot to make any more provision for ventilating that than the church, and it takes a pretty well–seasoned Christian to stay in it long at a time. The Sunday– school is held there, and it is thought to be best to accustom the children to bad air before they go into the church. The poor little dears shouldn't have the wickedness and impurity of this world break on them too suddenly. If the stranger noticed any lack about our church, it would be that of a spire. There is a place for one; indeed, it was begun, and then the builders seem to have stopped, with the notion that it would grow itself from such a good root. It is a mistake however, to suppose that we do not know that the church has what the profane here call a "stump–tail" appearance. But the profane are as ignorant of history as they are of true Gothic. All the Old World cathedrals were the work of centuries. That at Milan is scarcely finished yet; the unfinished spires of the Cologne cathedral are one of the best–known features of it. I doubt if it would be in the Gothic spirit to finish a church at once. We can tell cavilers that we shall have a spire at the proper time, and not a minute before. It may depend a little upon what the Baptists do, who are to build near us. I, for one, think we had better wait and see how high the Baptist spire is before we run ours up. The church is everything that could be desired inside. There is the nave, with its lofty and beautiful arched ceiling; there are the side aisles, and two elegant rows of stone pillars, stained so as to be a perfect imitation of stucco; there is the apse, with its stained glass and exquisite lines; and there is an organ–loft over the front entrance, with a rose window. Nothing was wanting, so far as we could see, except that we should adapt ourselves to the circumstances; and that we have been trying to do ever since. It may be well to relate how we do it, for the benefit of other inchoate Goths.

It was found that if we put up the organ in the loft, it would hide the beautiful rose window. Besides, we wanted congregational sing– ing, and if we hired a choir, and hung it up there under the roof, like a cage of birds, we should not have congregational singing. We therefore left the organ–loft vacant, making no further use of it than to satisfy our Gothic cravings. As for choir,—several of the singers of the church volunteered to sit together in the front side–seats, and as there was no place for an organ, they gallantly rallied round a melodeon,—or perhaps it is a cabinet organ,—a charming instrument, and, as everybody knows, entirely in keeping with the pillars, arches, and great spaces of a real Gothic edifice. It is the union of simplicity with grandeur, for which we have all been looking. I need not say to those who have ever heard a melodeon, that there is nothing like it. It is rare, even in the finest churches on the Continent. And we had congregational singing. And it went very well indeed. One of the advantages of pure congregational singing, is that you can join in the singing whether you have a voice or not. The disadvantage is, that your neighbor can do the same. It is strange what an uncommonly poor lot of voices there is, even among good people. But we enjoy it. If you do not enjoy it, you can change your seat until you get among a good lot.

So far, everything went well. But it was next discovered that it was difficult to hear the minister, who had a very handsome little desk in the apse, somewhat distant from the bulk of the congregation; still, we could most of us see him on a clear day. The church was admirably built for echoes, and the centre of the house was very favorable to them. When you sat in the centre of the house, it sometimes seemed as if three or four ministers were speaking.

It is usually so in cathedrals; the Right Reverend So–and–So is assisted by the very Reverend Such–and–Such, and the good deal Reverend Thus–and–Thus, and so on. But a good deal of the minister's voice appeared to go up into the groined arches, and, as there was no one up there, some of his best things were lost. We also had a notion that some of it went into the cavernous organ–loft. It would have been all right if there had been a choir there, for choirs usually need more preaching, and pay less heed to it, than any other part of the congregation. Well, we drew a sort of screen over the organ–loft; but the result was not as marked as we had hoped. We next devised a sounding–board,—a sort of mammoth clamshell, painted white,—and erected it behind the minister. It had a good effect on the minister. It kept him up straight to his work. So long as he kept his head exactly in the focus, his voice went out and did not return to him; but if he moved either way, he was assailed by a Babel of clamoring echoes. There was no opportunity for him to splurge about from side to side of the pulpit, as some do. And if he raised his voice much, or attempted any extra flights, he was liable to be drowned in a refluent sea of his own eloquence. And he could hear the congregation as well as they could hear him. All the coughs, whispers, noises, were gathered in the wooden tympanum behind him, and poured into his ears.

But the sounding–board was an improvement, and we advanced to bolder measures; having heard a little, we wanted to hear more. Besides, those who sat in front began to be discontented with the melodeon. There are depths in music which the melodeon, even when it is called a cabinet organ, with a colored boy at the bellows, cannot sound. The melodeon was not, originally, designed for the Gothic worship. We determined to have an organ, and we speculated whether, by erecting it in the apse, we could not fill up that elegant portion of the church, and compel the preacher's voice to leave it, and go out over the pews. It would of course do something to efface the main beauty of a Gothic church; but something must be done, and we began a series of experiments to test the probable effects of putting the organ and choir behind the minister. We moved the desk to the very front of the platform, and erected behind it a high, square board screen, like a section of tight fence round the fair–grounds. This did help matters. The minister spoke with more ease, and we could hear him better. If the screen had been intended to stay there, we should have agitated the subject of painting it. But this was only an experiment.

Our next move was to shove the screen back and mount the volunteer singers, melodeon and all, upon the platform,—some twenty of them crowded together behind the minister. The, effect was beautiful. It seemed as if we had taken care to select the finest–looking people in the congregation,—much to the injury of the congregation, of course, as seen from the platform. There are few congregations that can stand this sort of culling, though ours can endure it as well as any; yet it devolves upon those of us who remain the responsibility of looking as well as we can.

The experiment was a success, so far as appearances went, but when the screen went back, the minister's voice went back with it. We could not hear him very well, though we could hear the choir as plain as day. We have thought of remedying this last defect by putting the high screen in front of the singers, and close to the minister, as it was before. This would make the singers invisible,—"though lost to sight, to memory dear,"—what is sometimes called an "angel choir," when the singers (and the melodeon) are concealed, with the most subdued and religious effect. It is often so in cathedrals.

This plan would have another advantage. The singers on the platform, all handsome and well dressed, distract our attention from the minister, and what he is saying. We cannot help looking at them, studying all the faces and all the dresses. If one of them sits up very straight, he is a rebuke to us; if he "lops" over, we wonder why he does n't sit up; if his hair is white, we wonder whether it is age or family peculiarity; if he yawns, we want to yawn; if he takes up a hymn–book, we wonder if he is uninterested in the sermon; we look at the bonnets, and query if that is the latest spring style, or whether we are to look for another; if he shaves close, we wonder why he doesn't let his beard grow; if he has long whiskers, we wonder why he does n't trim 'em; if she sighs, we feel sorry; if she smiles, we would like to know what it is about. And, then, suppose any of the singers should ever want to eat fennel, or peppermints, or Brown's troches, and pass them round! Suppose the singers, more or less of them, should sneeze!

Suppose one or two of them, as the handsomest people sometimes will, should go to sleep! In short, the singers there take away all our attention from the minister, and would do so if they were the homeliest people in the world. We must try something else.

It is needless to explain that a Gothic religious life is not an idle one.

EIGHTH STUDY

I

Perhaps the clothes question is exhausted, philosophically. I cannot but regret that the Poet of the Breakfast–Table, who appears to have an uncontrollable penchant for saying the things you would like to say yourself, has alluded to the anachronism of "Sir Coeur de Lion Plantagenet in the mutton–chop whiskers and the plain gray suit."

Backlog Studies

A great many scribblers have felt the disadvantage of writing after Montaigne; and it is impossible to tell how much originality in others Dr. Holmes has destroyed in this country. In whist there are some men you always prefer to have on your left hand, and I take it that this intuitive essayist, who is so alert to seize the few remaining unappropriated ideas and analogies in the world, is one of them.

No doubt if the Plantagenets of this day were required to dress in a suit of chain–armor and wear iron pots on their heads, they would be as ridiculous as most tragedy actors on the stage. The pit which recognizes Snooks in his tin breastplate and helmet laughs at him, and Snooks himself feels like a sheep; and when the great tragedian comes on, shining in mail, dragging a two–handed sword, and mouths the grandiloquence which poets have put into the speech of heroes, the dress–circle requires all its good–breeding and its feigned love of the traditionary drama not to titter.

If this sort of acting, which is supposed to have come down to us from the Elizabethan age, and which culminated in the school of the Keans, Kembles, and Siddonses, ever had any fidelity to life, it must have been in a society as artificial as the prose of Sir Philip Sidney. That anybody ever believed in it is difficult to think, especially when we read what privileges the fine beaux and gallants of the town took behind the scenes and on the stage in the golden days of the drama. When a part of the audience sat on the stage, and gentlemen lounged or reeled across it in the midst of a play, to speak to acquaintances in the audience, the illusion could not have been very strong.

Now and then a genius, like Rachel as Horatia, or Hackett as Falstaff, may actually seem to be the character assumed by virtue of a transforming imagination, but I suppose the fact to be that getting into a costume, absurdly antiquated and remote from all the habits and associations of the actor, largely accounts for the incongruity and ridiculousness of most of our modern acting. Whether what is called the "legitimate drama" ever was legitimate we do not know, but the advocates of it appear to think that the theatre was some time cast in a mould, once for all, and is good for all times and peoples, like the propositions of Euclid. To our eyes the legitimate drama of to–day is the one in which the day is reflected, both in costume and speech, and which touches the affections, the passions, the humor, of the present time. The brilliant success of the few good plays that have been written out of the rich life which we now live—the most varied, fruitful, and dramatically suggestive—ought to rid us forever of the buskin–fustian, except as a pantomimic or spectacular curiosity.

We have no objection to Julius Caesar or Richard III. stalking about in impossible clothes) and stepping four feet at a stride, if they want to, but let them not claim to be more "legitimate" than "Ours" or "Rip Van Winkle." There will probably be some orator for years and years to come, at every Fourth of July, who will go on asking, Where is Thebes? but he does not care anything about it, and he does not really expect an answer. I have sometimes wished I knew the exact site of Thebes, so that I could rise in the audience, and stop that question, at any rate. It is legitimate, but it is tiresome.

If we went to the bottom of this subject, I think we should find that the putting upon actors clothes to which they are unaccustomed makes them act and talk artificially, and often in a manner intolerable.

An actor who has not the habits or instincts of a gentleman cannot be made to appear like one on the stage by dress; he only caricatures and discredits what he tries to represent; and the unaccustomed clothes and situation make him much more unnatural and insufferable than he would otherwise be. Dressed appropriately for parts for which he is fitted, he will act well enough, probably. What I mean is, that the clothes inappropriate to the man make the incongruity of him and his part more apparent. Vulgarity is never so conspicuous as in fine apparel, on or off the stage, and never so self-conscious. Shall we have, then, no refined characters on the stage? Yes; but let them be taken by men and women of taste and refinement and let us have done with this masquerading in false raiment, ancient and modern, which makes nearly every stage a travesty of nature and the whole theatre a painful pretension. We do not expect the modern theatre to be a place of instruction (that business is now turned over to the telegraphic operator, who is making a new language), but it may give amusement instead of torture, and do a little in satirizing folly and kindling love of home and country by the way.

This is a sort of summary of what we all said, and no one in particular is responsible for it; and in this it is like public opinion. The Parson, however, whose only experience of the theatre was the endurance of an oratorio once, was very cordial in his denunciation of the stage altogether.

MANDEVILLE. Yet, acting itself is delightful; nothing so entertains us as mimicry, the personation of character. We enjoy it in private. I confess that I am always pleased with the Parson in the character of grumbler. He would be an immense success on the stage. I don't know but the theatre will have to go back into the hands of the priests, who once controlled it.

THE PARSON. Scoffer!

MANDEVILLE. I can imagine how enjoyable the stage might be, cleared of all its traditionary nonsense, stilted language, stilted behavior, all the rubbish of false sentiment, false dress, and the manners of times that were both artificial and immoral, and filled with living characters, who speak the thought of to-day, with the wit and culture that are current to-day. I've seen private theatricals, where all the performers were persons of cultivation, that....

OUR NEXT DOOR. So have I. For something particularly cheerful, commend me to amateur theatricals. I have passed some melancholy hours at them.

MANDEVILLE. That's because the performers acted the worn stage plays, and attempted to do them in the manner they had seen on the stage. It is not always so.

THE FIRE-TENDER. I suppose Mandeville would say that acting has got into a mannerism which is well described as stagey, and is supposed to be natural to the stage; just as half the modern poets write in a recognized form of literary manufacture, without the least impulse from within, and not with the purpose of saying anything, but of turning out a piece of literary work. That's the reason we have so much poetry that impresses one like sets of faultless cabinet- furniture made by machinery.

THE PARSON. But you need n't talk of nature or naturalness in acting or in anything. I tell you nature is poor stuff. It can't go alone. Amateur acting—they get it up at church sociables nowadays—is apt to be as near nature as a school-boy's declamation. Acting is the Devil's art.

THE MISTRESS. Do you object to such innocent amusement?

MANDEVILLE. What the Parson objects to is, that he isn't amused.

THE PARSON. What's the use of objecting? It's the fashion of the day to amuse people into the kingdom of heaven.

Backlog Studies

HERBERT. The Parson has got us off the track. My notion about the stage is, that it keeps along pretty evenly with the rest of the world; the stage is usually quite up to the level of the audience. Assumed dress on the stage, since you were speaking of that, makes people no more constrained and self–conscious than it does off the stage.

THE MISTRESS. What sarcasm is coming now?

HERBERT. Well, you may laugh, but the world has n't got used to good clothes yet. The majority do not wear them with ease. People who only put on their best on rare and stated occasions step into an artificial feeling.

OUR NEXT DOOR. I wonder if that's the reason the Parson finds it so difficult to get hold of his congregation.

HERBERT. I don't know how else to account for the formality and vapidity of a set "party," where all the guests are clothed in a manner to which they are unaccustomed, dressed into a condition of vivid self–consciousness. The same people, who know each other perfectly well, will enjoy themselves together without restraint in their ordinary apparel. But nothing can be more artificial than the behavior of people together who rarely "dress up." It seems impossible to make the conversation as fine as the clothes, and so it dies in a kind of inane helplessness. Especially is this true in the country, where people have not obtained the mastery of their clothes that those who live in the city have. It is really absurd, at this stage of our civilization, that we should be so affected by such an insignificant accident as dress. Perhaps Mandeville can tell us whether this clothes panic prevails in the older societies.

THE PARSON. Don't. We've heard it; about its being one of the Englishman's thirty–nine articles that he never shall sit down to dinner without a dress–coat, and all that.

THE MISTRESS. I wish, for my part, that everybody who has time to eat a dinner would dress for that, the principal event of the day, and do respectful and leisurely justice to it.

THE YOUNG LADY. It has always seemed singular to me that men who work so hard to build elegant houses, and have good dinners, should take so little leisure to enjoy either.

MANDEVILLE. If the Parson will permit me, I should say that the chief clothes question abroad just now is, how to get any; and it is the same with the dinners.

II

It is quite unnecessary to say that the talk about clothes ran into the question of dress–reform, and ran out, of course. You cannot converse on anything nowadays that you do not run into some reform. The Parson says that everybody is intent on reforming everything but himself. We are all trying to associate ourselves to make everybody else behave as we do. Said—

OUR NEXT DOOR. Dress reform! As if people couldn't change their clothes without concert of action. Resolved, that nobody should put on a clean collar oftener than his neighbor does. I'm sick of every sort of reform. I should like to retrograde awhile. Let a dyspeptic ascertain that he can eat porridge three times a day and live, and straightway he insists that everybody ought to eat porridge and nothing else. I mean to get up a society every member of which shall be pledged to do just as he pleases.

THE PARSON. That would be the most radical reform of the day. That would be independence. If people dressed according to their means, acted according to their convictions, and avowed their opinions, it would revolutionize society.

OUR NEXT DOOR. I should like to walk into your church some Sunday and see the changes under such conditions.

THE PARSON. It might give you a novel sensation to walk in at any time. And I'm not sure but the church would suit your retrograde ideas. It's so Gothic that a Christian of the Middle Ages, if he were alive, couldn't see or hear in it.

HERBERT. I don't know whether these reformers who carry the world on their shoulders in such serious fashion, especially the little fussy fellows, who are themselves the standard of the regeneration they seek, are more ludicrous than pathetic.

THE FIRE–TENDER. Pathetic, by all means. But I don't know that they would be pathetic if they were not ludicrous. There are those reform singers who have been piping away so sweetly now for thirty years, with never any diminution of cheerful, patient enthusiasm; their hair growing longer and longer, their eyes brighter and brighter, and their faces, I do believe, sweeter and sweeter; singing always with the same constancy for the slave, for the drunkard, for the snufftaker, for the suffragist,—"There'sa–good–time–com–ing–boys (nothing offensive is intended by "boys," it is put in for euphony, and sung pianissimo, not to offend the suffragists), it's–almost–here." And what a brightening up of their faces there is when they say, "it's–al–most–here," not doubting for a moment that "it's" coming tomorrow; and the accompanying melodeon also wails its wheezy suggestion that "it's–al–most–here," that "good–time" (delayed so long, waiting perhaps for the invention of the melodeon) when we shall all sing and all play that cheerful instrument, and all vote, and none shall smoke, or drink, or eat meat, "boys." I declare it almost makes me cry to hear them, so touching is their faith in the midst of a jeer–ing world.

HERBERT. I suspect that no one can be a genuine reformer and not be ridiculous. I mean those who give themselves up to the unction of the reform.

THE MISTRESS. Does n't that depend upon whether the reform is large or petty?

THE FIRE–TENDER. I should say rather that the reforms attracted to them all the ridiculous people, who almost always manage to become the most conspicuous. I suppose that nobody dare write out all that was ludicrous in the great abolition movement. But it was not at all comical to those most zealous in it; they never could see—more's the pity, for thereby they lose much—the humorous side of their per– formances, and that is why the pathos overcomes one's sense of the absurdity of such people.

THE YOUNG LADY. It is lucky for the world that so many are willing to be absurd.

HERBERT. Well, I think that, in the main, the reformers manage to look out for themselves tolerably well. I knew once a lean and faithful agent of a great philanthropic scheme, who contrived to collect every year for the cause just enough to support him at a good hotel comfortably.

THE MISTRESS. That's identifying one's self with the cause.

MANDEVILLE. You remember the great free–soil convention at Buffalo, in 1848, when Van Buren was nominated. All the world of hope and discontent went there, with its projects of reform. There seemed to be no doubt, among hundreds that attended it, that if they could get a resolution passed that bread should be buttered on both sides, it would be so buttered. The platform provided for every want and every woe.

THE FIRE–TENDER. I remember. If you could get the millennium by political action, we should have had it then.

MANDEVILLE. We went there on the Erie Canal, the exciting and fashionable mode of travel in those days. I was a boy when we began the voyage. The boat was full of conventionists; all the talk was of what must be done there. I got the impression that as that boat–load went so would go the convention; and I was not alone in that feeling. I can never be grateful enough for one little scrubby fanatic who was on board, who spent most of his time in drafting resolutions and reading them privately to the passengers. He was a very enthusiastic, nervous, and somewhat dirty little man, who wore a woolen muffler about his throat, although it was summer; he had nearly lost his voice, and could only speak in a hoarse, disagreeable whisper, and he always carried a teacup about, containing some sticky compound which he stirred frequently with a spoon, and took, whenever he talked, in order to improve his voice. If he was separated from his cup for ten minutes, his whisper became inaudible. I greatly delighted in him, for I never saw any one who had so much enjoyment of his own importance. He was fond of telling what he would do if the conven–tion rejected such and such resolutions. He'd make it hot for them. I did n't know but he'd make them take his mixture. The convention had got to take a stand on tobacco, for one thing. He'd heard Gid–dings took snuff; he'd see. When we at length reached Buffalo he took his teacup and carpet–bag of resolutions and went ashore in a great hurry. I saw him once again in a cheap restaurant, whispering a resolution to another delegate, but he did n't appear in the con–vention. I have often wondered what became of him.

OUR NEXT DOOR. Probably he's consul somewhere. They mostly are.

THE FIRE–TENDER. After all, it's the easiest thing in the world to sit and sneer at eccentricities. But what a dead and uninteresting world it would be if we were all proper, and kept within the lines! Affairs would soon be reduced to mere machinery. There are moments, even days, when all interests and movements appear to be settled upon some universal plan of equilibrium; but just then some restless and absurd person is inspired to throw the machine out of gear. These individual eccentricities seem to be the special providences in the general human scheme.

HERBERT. They make it very hard work for the rest of us, who are disposed to go along peaceably and smoothly.

MANDEVILLE. And stagnate. I 'm not sure but the natural condition of this planet is war, and that when it is finally towed to its anchorage—if the universe has any harbor for worlds out of commission—it will look like the Fighting Temeraire in Turner's picture.

HERBERT. There is another thing I should like to understand: the tendency of people who take up one reform, perhaps a personal regeneration in regard to some bad habit, to run into a dozen other isms, and get all at sea in several vague and pernicious theories and practices.

MANDEVILLE. Herbert seems to think there is safety in a man's being anchored, even if it is to a bad habit.

HERBERT. Thank you. But what is it in human nature that is apt to carry a man who may take a step in personal reform into so many extremes?

OUR NEXT DOOR. Probably it's human nature.

HERBERT. Why, for instance, should a reformed drunkard (one of the noblest examples of victory over self) incline, as I have known the reformed to do, to spiritism, or a woman suffragist to "pantarchism" (whatever that is), and want to pull up all the roots of society, and expect them to grow in the air, like orchids; or a Graham—bread disciple become enamored of Communism?

MANDEVILLE. I know an excellent Conservative who would, I think, suit you; he says that he does not see how a man who indulges in the theory and practice of total abstinence can be a consistent believer in the Christian religion.

HERBERT. Well, I can understand what he means: that a person is bound to hold himself in conditions of moderation and control, using and not abusing the things of this world, practicing temperance, not retiring into a convent of artificial restrictions in order to escape the full responsibility of self—control. And yet his theory would certainly wreck most men and women. What does the Parson say?

THE PARSON. That the world is going crazy on the notion of individual ability. Whenever a man attempts to reform himself, or anybody else, without the aid of the Christian religion, he is sure to go adrift, and is pretty certain to be blown about by absurd theories, and shipwrecked on some pernicious ism.

THE FIRE–TENDER. I think the discussion has touched bottom.

III

I never felt so much the value of a house with a backlog in it as during the late spring; for its lateness was its main feature. Everybody was grumbling about it, as if it were something ordered from the tailor, and not ready on the day. Day after day it snowed, night after night it blew a gale from the northwest; the frost sunk deeper and deeper into the ground; there was a popular longing for spring that was almost a prayer; the weather bureau was active; Easter was set a week earlier than the year before, but nothing seemed to do any good. The robins sat under the evergreens, and piped in a disconsolate mood, and at last the bluejays came and scolded in the midst of the snow–storm, as they always do scold in any weather. The crocuses could n't be coaxed to come up, even with a pickaxe. I'm almost ashamed now to recall what we said of the weather only I think that people are no more accountable for what they say of the weather than for their remarks when their corns are stepped on.

We agreed, however, that, but for disappointed expectations and the prospect of late lettuce and peas, we were gaining by the fire as much as we were losing by the frost. And the Mistress fell to chanting the comforts of modern civilization.

THE FIRE–TENDER said he should like to know, by the way, if our civilization differed essentially from any other in anything but its comforts.

HERBERT. We are no nearer religious unity.

THE PARSON. We have as much war as ever.

MANDEVILLE. There was never such a social turmoil.

Backlog Studies

THE YOUNG LADY. The artistic part of our nature does not appear to have grown.

THE FIRE-TENDER. We are quarreling as to whether we are in fact radically different from the brutes.

HERBERT. Scarcely two people think alike about the proper kind of human government.

THE PARSON. Our poetry is made out of words, for the most part, and not drawn from the living sources.

OUR NEXT DOOR. And Mr. Cumming is uncorking his seventh phial. I never felt before what barbarians we are.

THE MISTRESS. Yet you won't deny that the life of the average man is safer and every way more comfortable than it was even a century ago.

THE FIRE-TENDER. But what I want to know is, whether what we call our civilization has done any thing more for mankind at large than to increase the ease and pleasure of living? Science has multiplied wealth, and facilitated intercourse, and the result is refinement of manners and a diffusion of education and information. Are men and women essentially changed, however? I suppose the Parson would say we have lost faith, for one thing.

MANDEVILLE. And superstition; and gained toleration.

HERBERT. The question is, whether toleration is anything but indifference.

THE PARSON. Everything is tolerated now but Christian orthodoxy.

THE FIRE-TENDER. It's easy enough to make a brilliant catalogue of external achievements, but I take it that real progress ought to be in man himself. It is not a question of what a man enjoys, but what he can produce. The best sculpture was executed two thousand years ago. The best paintings are several centuries old. We study the finest architecture in its ruins. The standards of poetry are Shakespeare, Homer, Isaiah, and David. The latest of the arts, music, culminated in composition, though not in execution, a century ago.

Backlog Studies

THE MISTRESS. Yet culture in music certainly distinguishes the civilization of this age. It has taken eighteen hundred years for the principles of the Christian religion to begin to be practically incorporated in government and in ordinary business, and it will take a long time for Beethoven to be popularly recognized; but there is growth toward him, and not away from him, and when the average culture has reached his height, some other genius will still more profoundly and delicately express the highest thoughts.

HERBERT. I wish I could believe it. The spirit of this age is expressed by the Calliope.

THE PARSON. Yes, it remained for us to add church–bells and cannon to the orchestra.

OUR NEXT DOOR. It's a melancholy thought to me that we can no longer express ourselves with the bass–drum; there used to be the whole of the Fourth of July in its patriotic throbs.

MANDEVILLE. We certainly have made great progress in one art,—that of war.

THE YOUNG LADY. And in the humane alleviations of the miseries of war.

THE FIRE–TENDER. The most discouraging symptom to me in our undoubted advance in the comforts and refinements of society is the facility with which men slip back into barbarism, if the artificial and external accidents of their lives are changed. We have always kept a fringe of barbarism on our shifting western frontier; and I think there never was a worse society than that in California and Nevada in their early days.

THE YOUNG LADY. That is because women were absent.

THE FIRE–TENDER. But women are not absent in London and New York, and they are conspicuous in the most exceptionable demonstrations of social anarchy. Certainly they were not wanting in Paris. Yes, there was a city widely accepted as the summit of our material civilization. No city was so beautiful, so luxurious, so safe, so well ordered for the comfort of living, and yet it needed only a month or two to make it a kind of pandemonium of savagery. Its citizens were the barbarians who destroyed its own monuments of civilization. I don't mean to say that there was no apology for what was done there in the deceit and fraud that preceded it, but I simply notice how ready the tiger was to appear, and how little restraint all the material civilization was to the beast.

Backlog Studies

THE MISTRESS. I can't deny your instances, and yet I somehow feel that pretty much all you have been saying is in effect untrue. Not one of you would be willing to change our civilization for any other. In your estimate you take no account, it seems to me, of the growth of charity.

MANDEVILLE. And you might add a recognition of the value of human life.

THE MISTRESS. I don't believe there was ever before diffused everywhere such an element of good–will, and never before were women so much engaged in philanthropic work.

THE PARSON. It must be confessed that one of the best signs of the times is woman's charity for woman. That certainly never existed to the same extent in any other civilization.

MANDEVILLE. And there is another thing that distinguishes us, or is beginning to. That is, the notion that you can do something more with a criminal than punish him; and that society has not done its duty when it has built a sufficient number of schools for one class, or of decent jails for another.

HERBERT. It will be a long time before we get decent jails.

MANDEVILLE. But when we do they will begin to be places of education and training as much as of punishment and disgrace. The public will provide teachers in the prisons as it now does in the common schools.

THE FIRE–TENDER. The imperfections of our methods and means of selecting those in the community who ought to be in prison are so great, that extra care in dealing with them becomes us. We are beginning to learn that we cannot draw arbitrary lines with infal– lible justice. Perhaps half those who are convicted of crimes are as capable of reformation as half those transgressors who are not convicted, or who keep inside the statutory law.

HERBERT. Would you remove the odium of prison?

THE FIRE–TENDER. No; but I would have criminals believe, and society believe, that in going to prison a man or woman does not pass an absolute line and go into a fixed state.

THE PARSON. That is, you would not have judgment and retribution begin in this world.

OUR NEXT DOOR. Don't switch us off into theology. I hate to go up in a balloon, or see any one else go.

HERBERT. Don't you think there is too much leniency toward crime and criminals, taking the place of justice, in these days?

THE FIRE–TENDER. There may be too much disposition to condone the crimes of those who have been considered respectable.

OUR NEXT DOOR. That is, scarcely anybody wants to see his friend hung.

MANDEVILLE. I think a large part of the bitterness of the condemned arises from a sense of the inequality with which justice is administered. I am surprised, in visiting jails, to find so few respectable–looking convicts.

OUR NEXT DOOR. Nobody will go to jail nowadays who thinks anything of himself.

THE FIRE–TENDER. When society seriously takes hold of the reformation of criminals (say with as much determination as it does to carry an election) this false leniency will disappear; for it partly springs from a feeling that punishment is unequal, and does not discriminate enough in individuals, and that society itself has no right to turn a man over to the Devil, simply because he shows a strong leaning that way. A part of the scheme of those who work for the reformation of criminals is to render punishment more certain, and to let its extent depend upon reformation. There is no reason why a professional criminal, who won't change his trade for an honest one, should have intervals of freedom in his prison life in which he is let loose to prey upon society. Criminals ought to be discharged, like insane patients, when they are cured.

OUR NEXT DOOR. It's a wonder to me, what with our multitudes of statutes and hosts of detectives, that we are any of us out of jail. I never come away from a visit to a State-prison without a new spasm of fear and virtue. The faculties for getting into jail seem to be ample. We want more organizations for keeping people out.

MANDEVILLE. That is the sort of enterprise the women are engaged in, the frustration of the criminal tendencies of those born in vice. I believe women have it in their power to regenerate the world morally.

THE PARSON. It's time they began to undo the mischief of their mother.

THE MISTRESS. The reason they have not made more progress is that they have usually confined their individual efforts to one man; they are now organizing for a general campaign.

THE FIRE-TENDER. I'm not sure but here is where the ameliorations of the conditions of life, which are called the comforts of this civilization, come in, after all, and distinguish the age above all others. They have enabled the finer powers of women to have play as they could not in a ruder age. I should like to live a hundred years and see what they will do.

HERBERT. Not much but change the fashions, unless they submit them- selves to the same training and discipline that men do.

I have no doubt that Herbert had to apologize for this remark afterwards in private, as men are quite willing to do in particular cases; it is only in general they are unjust. The talk drifted off into general and particular depreciation of other times. Mandeville described a picture, in which he appeared to have confidence, of a fight between an Iguanodon and a Megalosaurus, where these huge iron-clad brutes were represented chewing up different portions of each other's bodies in a forest of the lower cretaceous period. So far as he could learn, that sort of thing went on unchecked for hundreds of thousands of years, and was typical of the intercourse of the races of man till a comparatively recent period. There was also that gigantic swan, the Plesiosaurus; in fact, all the early brutes were disgusting. He delighted to think that even the lower animals had improved, both in appearance and disposition.

The conversation ended, therefore, in a very amicable manner, having been taken to a ground that nobody knew anything about.

NINTH STUDY

I

Can you have a backlog in July? That depends upon circumstances.

In northern New England it is considered a sign of summer when the housewives fill the fireplaces with branches of mountain laurel, and, later, with the feathery stalks of the asparagus. This is often, too, the timid expression of a tender feeling, under Puritanic repression, which has not sufficient vent in the sweet–william and hollyhock at the front door. This is a yearning after beauty and ornamentation which has no other means of gratifying itself

In the most rigid circumstances, the graceful nature of woman thus discloses itself in these mute expressions of an undeveloped taste. You may never doubt what the common flowers growing along the pathway to the front door mean to the maiden of many summers who tends them; —love and religion, and the weariness of an uneventful life. The sacredness of the Sabbath, the hidden memory of an unrevealed and unrequited affection, the slow years of gathering and wasting sweetness, are in the smell of the pink and the sweet–clover. These sentimental plants breathe something of the longing of the maiden who sits in the Sunday evenings of summer on the lonesome front doorstone, singing the hymns of the saints, and perennial as the myrtle that grows thereby.

Yet not always in summer, even with the aid of unrequited love and devotional feeling, is it safe to let the fire go out on the hearth, in our latitude. I remember when the last almost total eclipse of the sun happened in August, what a bone–piercing chill came over the world. Perhaps the imagination had something to do with causing the chill from that temporary hiding of the sun to feel so much more penetrating than that from the coming on of night, which shortly followed. It was impossible not to experience a shudder as of the approach of the Judgment Day, when the shadows were flung upon the green lawn, and we all stood in the wan light, looking unfamiliar to each other. The birds in the trees felt the spell. We could in fancy see those spectral camp–fires which men would build on the earth, if the sun should slow its fires down to about the brilliancy of the moon. It was a great relief to all of us to go into the house, and, before a blazing wood–fire, talk of the end of the world.

In New England it is scarcely ever safe to let the fire go out; it is best to bank it, for it needs but the turn of a weather–vane at any hour to sweep the

Atlantic rains over us, or to bring down the chill of Hudson's Bay. There are days when the steam ship on the Atlantic glides calmly along under a full canvas, but its central fires must always be ready to make steam against head–winds and antagonistic waves. Even in our most smiling summer days one needs to have the materials of a cheerful fire at hand. It is only by this readiness for a change that one can preserve an equal mind. We are made provident and sagacious by the fickleness of our climate. We should be another sort of people if we could have that serene, unclouded trust in nature which the Egyptian has. The gravity and repose of the Eastern peoples is due to the unchanging aspect of the sky, and the deliberation and reg–ularity of the great climatic processes. Our literature, politics, religion, show the effect of unsettled weather. But they compare favorably with the Egyptian, for all that.

II

You cannot know, the Young Lady wrote, with what longing I look back to those winter days by the fire; though all the windows are open to this May morning, and the brown thrush is singing in the chestnut– tree, and I see everywhere that first delicate flush of spring, which seems too evanescent to be color even, and amounts to little more than a suffusion of the atmosphere. I doubt, indeed, if the spring is exactly what it used to be, or if, as we get on in years [no one ever speaks of "getting on in years" till she is virtually settled in life], its promises and suggestions do not seem empty in comparison with the sympathies and responses of human friendship, and the stimulation of society. Sometimes nothing is so tiresome as a perfect day in a perfect season.

I only imperfectly understand this. The Parson says that woman is always most restless under the most favorable conditions, and that there is no state in which she is really happy except that of change. I suppose this is the truth taught in what has been called the "Myth of the Garden." Woman is perpetual revolution, and is that element in the world which continually destroys and re–creates. She is the experimenter and the suggester of

93

new combinations. She has no belief in any law of eternal fitness of things. She is never even content with any arrangement of her own house. The only reason the Mistress could give, when she rearranged her apartment, for hanging a picture in what seemed the most inappropriate place, was that it had never been there before. Woman has no respect for tradition, and because a thing is as it is is sufficient reason for changing it. When she gets into law, as she has come into literature, we shall gain something in the destruction of all our vast and musty libraries of precedents, which now fetter our administration of individual justice. It is Mandeville's opinion that women are not so sentimental as men, and are not so easily touched with the unspoken poetry of nature; being less poetical, and having less imagination, they are more fitted for practical affairs, and would make less failures in business. I have noticed the almost selfish passion for their flowers which old gardeners have, and their reluctance to part with a leaf or a blossom from their family. They love the flowers for themselves. A woman raises flowers for their use. She is destruct−ion in a conservatory. She wants the flowers for her lover, for the sick, for the poor, for the Lord on Easter day, for the ornamentation of her house. She delights in the costly pleasure of sacrificing them. She never sees a flower but she has an intense but probably sinless desire to pick it.

It has been so from the first, though from the first she has been thwarted by the accidental superior strength of man. Whatever she has obtained has been by craft, and by the same coaxing which the sun uses to draw the blossoms out of the apple−trees. I am not surprised to learn that she has become tired of indulgences, and wants some of the original rights. We are just beginning to find out the extent to which she has been denied and subjected, and especially her condition among the primitive and barbarous races. I have never seen it in a platform of grievances, but it is true that among the Fijians she is not, unless a better civilization has wrought a change in her behalf, permitted to eat people, even her own sex, at the feasts of the men; the dainty enjoyed by the men being considered too good to be wasted on women. Is anything wanting to this picture of the degradation of woman? By a refinement of cruelty she receives no benefit whatever from the missionaries who are sent out by—what to her must seem a new name for Tantalus—the American Board.

I suppose the Young Lady expressed a nearly universal feeling in her regret at the breaking up of the winter−fireside company. Society needs a certain seclusion and the sense of security. Spring opens the doors and the windows, and the noise and unrest of the world are let in. Even a winter thaw begets a desire to travel, and summer brings longings innumerable, and disturbs the most tranquil souls. Nature is, in fact, a suggester of uneasiness, a promoter of pilgrimages and of excursions of the fancy which never come to any satisfactory haven. The summer in these latitudes is a campaign of sentiment and a season, for the most part, of restlessness and discontent. We grow now in hot—houses roses which, in form and color, are magnificent, and appear to be full of passion; yet one simple June rose of the open air has for the Young Lady, I doubt not, more sentiment and suggestion of love than a conservatory full of them in January. And this suggestion, leavened as it is with the inconstancy of nature, stimulated by the promises which are so often like the peach—blossom of the Judas—tree, unsatisfying by reason of its vague possibilities, differs so essentially from the more limited and attainable and home—like emotion born of quiet intercourse by the winter fireside, that I do not wonder the Young Lady feels as if some spell had been broken by the transition of her life from in—doors to out—doors. Her secret, if secret she has, which I do not at all know, is shared by the birds and the new leaves and the blossoms on the fruit trees. If we lived elsewhere, in that zone where the poets pretend always to dwell, we might be content, perhaps I should say drugged, by the sweet influences of an unchanging summer; but not living elsewhere, we can understand why the Young Lady probably now looks forward to the hearthstone as the most assured center of enduring attachment.

If it should ever become the sad duty of this biographer to write of disappointed love, I am sure he would not have any sensational story to tell of the Young Lady. She is one of those women whose unostentatious lives are the chief blessing of humanity; who, with a sigh heard only by herself and no change in her sunny face, would put behind her all the memories of winter evenings and the promises of May mornings, and give her life to some ministration of human kindness with an assiduity that would make her occupation appear like an election and a first choice. The disappointed man scowls, and hates his race, and threatens self—destruction, choosing oftener the flowing bowl than the dagger, and becoming a reeling nuisance in the world. It would be much more manly in him to become the secretary of a Dorcas society.

I suppose it is true that women work for others with less expectation of reward than men, and give themselves to labors of self—sacrifice with much less thought of self. At least, this is true unless woman goes into some public performance, where notoriety has its attractions, and mounts some cause, to ride it man—fashion, when I think she becomes just as eager for applause and just as willing that self—sacrifice should result in self—elevation as man. For her, usually, are not those unbought—presentations which are forced upon firemen, philanthropists, legislators, railroad—men, and the superintendents of the moral instruction of the young. These are almost always pleasing and unexpected tributes to worth and modesty, and must be received with satisfaction when the public service rendered has not been with a view to procuring them. We should say that one ought to be most liable to receive a "testimonial" who, being a superintendent of any sort, did not superintend with a view to getting it. But "testimonials" have become so common that a modest man ought really to be afraid to do his simple duty, for fear his motives will be misconstrued. Yet there are instances of very worthy men who have had things publicly presented to them. It is the blessed age of gifts and the reward of private virtue. And the presentations have become so frequent that we wish there were a little more variety in them. There never was much sense in giving a gallant fellow a big speaking—trumpet to carry home to aid him in his intercourse with his family; and the festive ice—pitcher has become a too universal sign of absolute devotion to the public interest. The lack of one will soon be proof that a man is a knave. The legislative cane with the gold head, also, is getting to be recognized as the sign of the immaculate public servant, as the inscription on it testifies, and the steps of suspicion must ere—long dog him who does not carry one. The "testimonial" business is, in truth, a little demoralizing, almost as much so as the "donation;" and the demoralization has extended even to our language, so that a perfectly respectable man is often obliged to see himself "made the recipient of" this and that. It would be much better, if testimonials must be, to give a man a barrel of flour or a keg of oysters, and let him eat himself at once back into the ranks of ordinary men.

III

We may have a testimonial class in time, a sort of nobility here in America, made so by popular gift, the members of which will all be able to show some stick or piece of plated ware or massive chain, "of which they have been the recipients." In time it may be a distinction not to belong to it, and it may come to be thought more blessed to give than to receive. For it must have been remarked that it is not always to the cleverest and the most amiable and modest man that the deputation comes with the inevitable ice—pitcher (and "salver to match"), which has in it the magic and subtle quality of making the hour in which it is received the proudest of one's life. There has not been discovered any method of rewarding all the deserving people and bringing their virtues into the prominence of notoriety. And, indeed, it would be an unreasonable world if there had, for its chief charm and sweetness lie in the excellences in it which are reluctantly disclosed; one of the chief pleasures of living is in the daily discovery of good traits, nobilities, and kindliness both in those we have long known and in the chance passenger whose way happens for a day to lie with ours. The longer I live the more I am impressed with the excess of human kindness over human hatred, and the greater willingness to oblige than to disoblige that one meets at every turn. The selfishness in politics, the jealousy in letters, the bickering in art, the bitterness in theology, are all as nothing compared to the sweet charities, sacrifices, and deferences of private life. The people are few whom to know intimately is to dislike. Of course you want to hate somebody, if you can, just to keep your powers of discrimination bright, and to save yourself from becoming a mere mush of good–nature; but perhaps it is well to hate some historical person who has been dead so long as to be indifferent to it. It is more comfortable to hate people we have never seen. I cannot but think that Judas Iscariot has been of great service to the world as a sort of buffer for moral indignation which might have made a collision nearer home but for his utilized treachery. I used to know a venerable and most amiable gentleman and scholar, whose hospitable house was always overrun with wayside ministers, agents, and philanthropists, who loved their fellow–men better than they loved to work for their living; and he, I suspect, kept his moral balance even by indulgence in violent but most distant dislikes. When I met him casually in the street, his first salutation was likely to be such as this: "What a liar that Alison was! Don't you hate him?" And then would follow specifications of historical inveracity enough to make one's blood run cold. When he was thus discharged of his hatred by such a conductor, I presume he had not a spark left for those whose mission was partly to live upon him and other generous souls.

Mandeville and I were talking of the unknown people, one rainy night by the fire, while the Mistress was fitfully and interjectionally playing with the piano–keys in an improvising mood. Mandeville has a good deal of sentiment about him, and without any effort talks so beautifully sometimes that I constantly regret I cannot report his language. He has, besides, that sympathy of presence—I believe it is called magnetism by those who regard the brain as only a sort of galvanic battery—which makes it a greater pleasure to see him think, if I may say so, than to hear some people talk.

It makes one homesick in this world to think that there are so many rare people he can never know; and so many excellent people that scarcely any one will know, in fact. One discovers a friend by chance, and cannot but feel regret that twenty or thirty years of life maybe have been spent without the least knowledge of him. When he is once known, through him opening is made into another little world, into a circle of culture and loving hearts and enthusiasm in a dozen congenial pursuits, and prejudices perhaps. How instantly and easily the bachelor doubles his world when he marries, and enters into the unknown fellowship of the to him continually increasing company which is known in popular language as "all his wife's relations."

Near at hand daily, no doubt, are those worth knowing intimately, if one had the time and the opportunity. And when one travels he sees what a vast material there is for society and friendship, of which he can never avail himself. Car-load after car-load of summer travel goes by one at any railway-station, out of which he is sure he could choose a score of life-long friends, if the conductor would introduce him. There are faces of refinement, of quick wit, of sympathetic kindness,—interesting people, traveled people, entertaining people, —as you would say in Boston, "nice people you would admire to know," whom you constantly meet and pass without a sign of recognition, many of whom are no doubt your long-lost brothers and sisters. You can see that they also have their worlds and their interests, and they probably know a great many "nice" people. The matter of personal liking and attachment is a good deal due to the mere fortune of association. More fast friendships and pleasant acquaintanceships are formed on the Atlantic steamships between those who would have been only indifferent acquaintances elsewhere, than one would think possible on a voyage which naturally makes one as selfish as he is indifferent to his personal appearance. The Atlantic is the only power on earth I know that can make a woman indifferent to her personal appearance.

Mandeville remembers, and I think without detriment to himself, the glimpses he had in the White Mountains once of a young lady of whom his utmost efforts could give him no further information than her name. Chance sight of her on a passing stage or amid a group on some mountain lookout was all he ever had, and he did not even know certainly whether she was the perfect beauty and the lovely character he thought her. He said he would have known her, however, at a great distance; there was to her form that command of which we hear so much and which turns out to be nearly all command after the "ceremony;" or perhaps it was something in the glance of her eye or the turn of her head, or very likely it was a sweet inherited reserve or hauteur that captivated him, that filled his days with the expectation of seeing her, and made him hasten to the hotel-registers in the hope that her name was there recorded. Whatever it was, she interested him as one of the people he would like to know; and it piqued him that there was a life, rich in friendships, no doubt, in tastes, in many noblenesses, one of thousands of such, that must be absolutely nothing to him,—nothing but a window into heaven momentarily opened and then closed. I have myself no idea that she was a countess incognito, or that she had descended from any greater heights than those where Mandeville saw her, but I have always regretted that she went her way so mysteriously and left no glow, and that we shall wear out the remainder of our days without her society. I have looked for her name, but always in vain, among the attendants at the rights– conventions, in the list of those good Americans presented at court, among those skeleton names that appear as the remains of beauty in the morning journals after a ball to the wandering prince, in the reports of railway collisions and steamboat explosions. No news comes of her. And so imperfect are our means of communication in this world that, for anything we know, she may have left it long ago by some private way.

IV

The lasting regret that we cannot know more of the bright, sincere, and genuine people of the world is increased by the fact that they are all different from each other. Was it not Madame de Sevigne who said she had loved several different women for several different qualities? Every real person—for there are persons as there are fruits that have no distinguishing flavor, mere gooseberries—has a distinct quality, and the finding it is always like the discovery of a new island to the voyager. The physical world we shall exhaust some day, having a written description of every foot of it to which we can turn; but we shall never get the different qualities of people into a biographical dictionary, and the making acquaintance with a human being will never cease to be an exciting experiment. We cannot even classify men so as to aid us much in our estimate of them. The efforts in this direction are ingenious, but unsatisfactory. If I hear that a man is lymphatic or nervous–sanguine, I cannot tell therefrom whether I shall like and trust him. He may produce a phrenological chart showing that his knobby head is the home of all the virtues, and that the vicious tendencies are represented by holes in his cranium, and yet I cannot be sure that he will not be as disagreeable as if phrenology had not been invented. I feel sometimes that phrenology is the refuge of mediocrity. Its charts are almost as misleading concerning character as photographs. And photography may be described as the art which enables commonplace mediocrity to look like genius. The heavy–jowled man with shallow cerebrum has only to incline his head so that the lying instrument can select a favorable focus, to appear in the picture with the brow of a sage and the chin of a poet. Of all the arts for ministering to human vanity the photographic is the most useful, but it is a poor aid in the revelation of character. You shall learn more of a man's real nature by seeing him walk once up the broad aisle of his church to his pew on Sunday, than by studying his photograph for a month.

No, we do not get any certain standard of men by a chart of their temperaments; it will hardly answer to select a wife by the color of her hair; though it be by nature as red as a cardinal's hat, she may be no more constant than if it were dyed. The farmer who shuns all the lymphatic beauties in his neighborhood, and selects to wife the most nervous−sanguine, may find that she is unwilling to get up in the winter mornings and make the kitchen fire. Many a man, even in this scientific age which professes to label us all, has been cruelly deceived in this way. Neither the blondes nor the brunettes act according to the advertisement of their temperaments. The truth is that men refuse to come under the classifications of the pseudo− scientists, and all our new nomenclatures do not add much to our knowledge. You know what to expect—if the comparison will be pardoned—of a horse with certain points; but you wouldn't dare go on a journey with a man merely upon the strength of knowing that his temperament was the proper mixture of the sanguine and the phlegmatic. Science is not able to teach us concerning men as it teaches us of horses, though I am very far from saying that there are not traits of nobleness and of meanness that run through families and can be calculated to appear in individuals with absolute certainty; one family will be trusty and another tricky through all its members for generations; noble strains and ignoble strains are perpetuated. When we hear that she has eloped with the stable−boy and married him, we are apt to remark, "Well, she was a Bogardus." And when we read that she has gone on a mission and has died, distinguishing herself by some extraordinary devotion to the heathen at Ujiji, we think it sufficient to say, "Yes, her mother married into the Smiths." But this knowledge comes of our experience of special families, and stands us in stead no further.

If we cannot classify men scientifically and reduce them under a kind of botanical order, as if they had a calculable vegetable development, neither can we gain much knowledge of them by comparison. It does not help me at all in my estimate of their characters to compare Mandeville with the Young Lady, or Our Next Door with the Parson. The wise man does not permit himself to set up even in his own mind any comparison of his friends. His friendship is capable of going to extremes with many people, evoked as it is by many qualities. When Mandeville goes into my garden in June I can usually find him in a particular bed of strawberries, but he does not speak disrespectfully of the others. When Nature, says Mandeville, consents to put herself into any sort of strawberry, I have no criticisms to make, I am only glad that I have been created into the same world with such a delicious manifestation of the Divine favor. If I left Mandeville alone in the garden long enough, I have no doubt he would impartially make an end of the fruit of all the beds, for his capacity in this direction is as all–embracing as it is in the matter of friendships. The Young Lady has also her favorite patch of berries. And the Parson, I am sorry to say, prefers to have them picked for him the elect of the garden—and served in an orthodox manner. The straw–berry has a sort of poetical precedence, and I presume that no fruit is jealous of it any more than any flower is jealous of the rose; but I remark the facility with which liking for it is transferred to the raspberry, and from the raspberry (not to make a tedious enumeration) to the melon, and from the melon to the grape, and the grape to the pear, and the pear to the apple. And we do not mar our enjoyment of each by comparisons.

Of course it would be a dull world if we could not criticise our friends, but the most unprofitable and unsatisfactory criticism is that by comparison. Criticism is not necessarily uncharitableness, but a wholesome exercise of our powers of analysis and discrimination. It is, however, a very idle exercise, leading to no results when we set the qualities of one over against the qualities of another, and disparage by contrast and not by independent judgment. And this method of procedure creates jealousies and heart–burnings innumerable.

Criticism by comparison is the refuge of incapables, and especially is this true in literature. It is a lazy way of disposing of a young poet to bluntly declare, without any sort of discrimination of his defects or his excellences, that he equals Tennyson, and that Scott never wrote anything finer. What is the justice of damning a meritorious novelist by comparing him with Dickens, and smothering him with thoughtless and good–natured eulogy? The poet and the novelist may be well enough, and probably have qualities and gifts of their own which are worth the critic's attention, if he has any time to bestow on them; and it is certainly unjust to subject them to a comparison with somebody else, merely because the critic will not take the trouble to ascertain what they are. If, indeed, the poet and novelist are mere imitators of a model and copyists of a style, they may be dismissed with such commendation as we bestow upon the machines who pass their lives in making bad copies of the pictures of the great painters. But the critics of whom we speak do not intend depreciation, but eulogy, when they say that the author they have in hand has the wit of Sydney Smith and the brilliancy of Macaulay. Probably he is not like either of them, and may have a genuine though modest virtue of his own; but these names will certainly kill him, and he will never be anybody in the popular estimation. The public finds out speedily that he is not Sydney Smith, and it resents the extravagant claim for him as if he were an impudent pretender. How many authors of fair ability to interest the world have we known in our own day who have been thus sky—rocketed into notoriety by the lazy indiscrimination of the critic—by—comparison, and then have sunk into a popular contempt as undeserved! I never see a young aspirant injudiciously compared to a great and resplendent name in literature, but I feel like saying, My poor fellow, your days are few and full of trouble; you begin life handicapped, and you cannot possibly run a creditable race.

I think this sort of critical eulogy is more damaging even than that which kills by a different assumption, and one which is equally common, namely, that the author has not done what he probably never intended to do. It is well known that most of the trouble in life comes from our inability to compel other people to do what we think they ought, and it is true in criticism that we are unwilling to take a book for what it is, and credit the author with that. When the solemn critic, like a mastiff with a ladies' bonnet in his mouth, gets hold of a light piece of verse, or a graceful sketch which catches the humor of an hour for the entertainment of an hour, he tears it into a thousand shreds. It adds nothing to human knowledge, it solves none of the problems of life, it touches none of the questions of social science, it is not a philosophical treatise, and it is not a dozen things that it might have been. The critic cannot forgive the author for this disrespect to him. This isn't a rose, says the critic, taking up a pansy and rending it; it is not at all like a rose, and the author is either a pretentious idiot or an idiotic pretender. What business, indeed, has the author to send the critic a bunch of sweet—peas, when he knows that a cabbage would be preferred,—something not showy, but useful?

A good deal of this is what Mandeville said and I am not sure that it is devoid of personal feeling. He published, some years ago, a little volume giving an account of a trip through the Great West, and a very entertaining book it was. But one of the heavy critics got hold of it, and made Mandeville appear, even to himself, he confessed, like an ass, because there was nothing in the volume about geology or mining prospects, and very little to instruct the student of physical geography. With alternate sarcasm and ridicule, he literally basted the author, till Mandeville said that he felt almost like a depraved scoundrel, and thought he should be held up to less execration if he had committed a neat and scientific murder.

But I confess that I have a good deal of sympathy with the critics. Consider what these public tasters have to endure! None of us, I fancy, would like to be compelled to read all that they read, or to take into our mouths, even with the privilege of speedily ejecting it with a grimace, all that they sip. The critics of the vintage, who pursue their calling in the dark vaults and amid mouldy casks, give their opinion, for the most part, only upon wine, upon juice that has matured and ripened into development of quality. But what crude, unrestrained, unfermented—even raw and drugged liquor, must the literary taster put to his unwilling lips day after day!

TENTH STUDY

I

It was my good fortune once to visit a man who remembered the rebellion of 1745. Lest this confession should make me seem very aged, I will add that the visit took place in 1851, and that the man was then one hundred and thirteen years old. He was quite a lad before Dr. Johnson drank Mrs. Thrale's tea. That he was as old as he had the credit of being, I have the evidence of my own senses (and I am seldom mistaken in a person's age), of his own family, and his own word; and it is incredible that so old a person, and one so apparently near the grave, would deceive about his age.

The testimony of the very aged is always to be received without question, as Alexander Hamilton once learned. He was trying a land–title with Aaron Burr, and two of the witnesses upon whom Burr relied were venerable Dutchmen, who had, in their youth, carried the surveying chains over the land in dispute, and who were now aged respectively one hundred and four years and one hundred and six years. Hamilton gently attempted to undervalue their testimony, but he was instantly put down by the Dutch justice, who suggested that Mr. Hamilton could not be aware of the age of the witnesses.

My old man (the expression seems familiar and inelegant) had indeed an exaggerated idea of his own age, and sometimes said that he supposed he was going on four hundred, which was true enough, in fact; but for the exact date, he referred to his youngest son,—a frisky and humorsome lad of eighty years, who had received us at the gate, and whom we had at first mistaken for the veteran, his father. But when we beheld the old man, we saw the difference between age and age. The latter had settled into a grizzliness and grimness which belong to a very aged and stunted but sturdy oak–tree, upon the bark of which the gray moss is thick and heavy. The old man appeared hale enough, he could walk about, his sight and hearing were not seriously impaired, he ate with relish) and his teeth were so sound that he would not need a dentist for at least another century; but the moss was growing on him. His boy of eighty seemed a green sapling beside him.

He remembered absolutely nothing that had taken place within thirty years, but otherwise his mind was perhaps as good as it ever was, for he must always have been an ignoramus, and would never know anything if he lived to be as old as he said he was going on to be. Why he was interested in the rebellion of 1745 I could not discover, for he of course did not go over to Scotland to carry a pike in it, and he only remembered to have heard it talked about as a great event in the Irish market–town near which he lived, and to which he had ridden when a boy. And he knew much more about the horse that drew him, and the cart in which he rode, than he did about the rebellion of the Pretender.

I hope I do not appear to speak harshly of this amiable old man, and if he is still living I wish him well, although his example was bad in some respects. He had used tobacco for nearly a century, and the habit has very likely been the death of him. If so, it is to be regretted. For it would have been interesting to watch the process of his gradual disintegration and return to the ground: the loss of sense after sense, as decaying limbs fall from the oak; the failure of discrimination, of the power of choice, and finally of memory itself; the peaceful wearing out and passing away of body and mind without disease, the natural running down of a man. The interesting fact about him at that time was that his bodily powers seemed in sufficient vigor, but that the mind had not force enough to manifest itself through his organs. The complete battery was there, the appetite was there, the acid was eating the zinc; but the electric current was too weak to flash from the brain. And yet he appeared so sound throughout, that it was difficult to say that his mind was not as good as it ever had been. He had stored in it very little to feed on, and any mind would get enfeebled by a century's rumination on a hearsay idea of the rebellion of '45.

It was possible with this man to fully test one's respect for age, which is in all civilized nations a duty. And I found that my feelings were mixed about him. I discovered in him a conceit in regard to his long sojourn on this earth, as if it were somehow a credit to him. In the presence of his good opinion of himself, I could but question the real value of his continued life) to himself or to others. If he ever had any friends he had outlived them, except his boy; his wives—a century of them—were all dead; the world had actually passed away for him. He hung on the tree like a frost–nipped apple, which the farmer has neglected to gather. The world always renews itself, and remains young. What relation had he to it?

I was delighted to find that this old man had never voted for George Washington. I do not know that he had ever heard of him. Washington may be said to have played his part since his time. I am not sure that he perfectly remembered anything so recent as the American Revolution. He was living quietly in Ireland during our French and Indian wars, and he did not emigrate to this country till long after our revolutionary and our constitutional struggles were over. The Rebellion Of '45 was the great event of the world for him, and of that he knew nothing.

I intend no disrespect to this man,—a cheerful and pleasant enough old person,—but he had evidently lived himself out of the world, as completely as people usually die out of it. His only remaining value was to the moralist, who might perchance make something out of him. I suppose if he had died young, he would have been regretted, and his friends would have lamented that he did not fill out his days in the world, and would very likely have called him back, if tears and prayers could have done so. They can see now what his prolonged life amounted to, and how the world has closed up the gap he once filled while he still lives in it.

A great part of the unhappiness of this world consists in regret for those who depart, as it seems to us, prematurely. We imagine that if they would return, the old conditions would be restored. But would it be so? If they, in any case, came back, would there be any place for them? The world so quickly readjusts itself after any loss, that the return of the departed would nearly always throw it, even the circle most interested, into confusion. Are the Enoch Ardens ever wanted?

II

A popular notion akin to this, that the world would have any room for the departed if they should now and then return, is the constant regret that people will not learn by the experience of others, that one generation learns little from the preceding, and that youth never will adopt the experience of age. But if experience went for anything, we should all come to a standstill; for there is nothing so discouraging to effort. Disbelief in Ecclesiastes is the mainspring of action. In that lies the freshness and the interest of life, and it is the source of every endeavor.

Backlog Studies

If the boy believed that the accumulation of wealth and the acquisition of power were what the old man says they are, the world would very soon be stagnant. If he believed that his chances of obtaining either were as poor as the majority of men find them to be, ambition would die within him. It is because he rejects the experience of those who have preceded him, that the world is kept in the topsy–turvy condition which we all rejoice in, and which we call progress.

And yet I confess I have a soft place in my heart for that rare character in our New England life who is content with the world as he finds it, and who does not attempt to appropriate any more of it to himself than he absolutely needs from day to day. He knows from the beginning that the world could get on without him, and he has never had any anxiety to leave any result behind him, any legacy for the world to quarrel over.

He is really an exotic in our New England climate and society, and his life is perpetually misunderstood by his neighbors, because he shares none of their uneasiness about getting on in life. He is even called lazy, good–for–nothing, and "shiftless,"—the final stigma that we put upon a person who has learned to wait without the exhausting process of laboring.

I made his acquaintance last summer in the country, and I have not in a long time been so well pleased with any of our species. He was a man past middle life, with a large family. He had always been from boyhood of a contented and placid mind, slow in his movements, slow in his speech. I think he never cherished a hard feeling toward anybody, nor envied any one, least of all the rich and prosperous about whom he liked to talk. Indeed, his talk was a good deal about wealth, especially about his cousin who had been down South and "got fore–handed" within a few years. He was genuinely pleased at his relation's good luck, and pointed him out to me with some pride. But he had no envy of him, and he evinced no desire to imitate him. I inferred from all his conversation about "piling it up" (of which he spoke with a gleam of enthusiasm in his eye), that there were moments when he would like to be rich himself; but it was evident that he would never make the least effort to be so, and I doubt if he could even overcome that delicious inertia of mind and body called laziness, sufficiently to inherit.

Wealth seemed to have a far and peculiar fascination for him, and I suspect he was a visionary in the midst of his poverty. Yet I suppose he had—hardly the personal property which the law exempts from execution. He had lived in a great many towns, moving from one to another with his growing family, by easy stages, and was always the poorest man in the town, and lived on the most niggardly of its rocky and bramble–grown farms, the productiveness of which he reduced to zero in a couple of seasons by his careful neglect of culture. The fences of his hired domain always fell into ruins under him, perhaps because he sat on them so much, and the hovels he occupied rotted down during his placid residence in them. He moved from desolation to desolation, but carried always with him the equal mind of a philosopher. Not even the occasional tart remarks of his wife, about their nomadic life and his serenity in the midst of discomfort, could ruffle his smooth spirit.

He was, in every respect, a most worthy man, truthful, honest, temperate, and, I need not say, frugal; and he had no bad habits,— perhaps he never had energy enough to acquire any. Nor did he lack the knack of the Yankee race. He could make a shoe, or build a house, or doctor a cow; but it never seemed to him, in this brief existence, worth while to do any of these things. He was an excellent angler, but he rarely fished; partly because of the shortness of days, partly on account of the uncertainty of bites, but principally because the trout brooks were all arranged lengthwise and ran over so much ground. But no man liked to look at a string of trout better than he did, and he was willing to sit down in a sunny place and talk about trout–fishing half a day at a time, and he would talk pleasantly and well too, though his wife might be continually interrupting him by a call for firewood.

I should not do justice to his own idea of himself if I did not add that he was most respectably connected, and that he had a justifiable though feeble pride in his family. It helped his self–respect, which no ignoble circumstances could destroy. He was, as must appear by this time, a most intelligent man, and he was a well–informed man; that is to say, he read the weekly newspapers when he could get them, and he had the average country information about Beecher and Greeley and the Prussian war (" Napoleon is gettin' on't, ain't he?"), and the general prospect of the election campaigns. Indeed, he was warmly, or rather luke–warmly, interested in politics. He liked to talk about the inflated currency, and it seemed plain to him that his condition would somehow be improved if we could get to a specie basis. He was, in fact, a little troubled by the national debt; it seemed to press on him somehow, while his own never did. He exhibited more animation over the affairs of the government than he did over his own,—an evidence at once of his disinterestedness and his patriotism. He had been an old abolitionist, and was strong on the rights of free labor, though he did not care to exercise his privilege much. Of course he had the proper contempt for the poor whites down South. I never saw a person with more correct notions on such a variety of subjects. He was perfectly willing that churches (being himself a member), and Sunday–schools, and missionary enterprises should go on; in fact, I do not believe he ever opposed anything in his life. No one was more willing to vote town taxes and road–repairs and schoolhouses than he. If you could call him spirited at all, he was public–spirited.

And with all this he was never very well; he had, from boyhood, "enjoyed poor health." You would say he was not a man who would ever catch anything, not even an epidemic; but he was a person whom diseases would be likely to overtake, even the slowest of slow fevers. And he was n't a man to shake off anything. And yet sickness seemed to trouble him no more than poverty. He was not discontented; he never grumbled. I am not sure but he relished a "spell of sickness" in haying–time.

An admirably balanced man, who accepts the world as it is, and evidently lives on the experience of others. I have never seen a man with less envy, or more cheerfulness, or so contented with as little reason for being so. The only drawback to his future is that rest beyond the grave will not be much change for him, and he has no works to follow him.

III

This Yankee philosopher, who, without being a Brahmin, had, in an uncongenial atmosphere, reached the perfect condition of Nirvina, reminded us all of the ancient sages; and we queried whether a world that could produce such as he, and could, beside, lengthen a man's years to one hundred and thirteen, could fairly be called an old and worn–out world, having long passed the stage of its primeval poetry and simplicity. Many an Eastern dervish has, I think, got immortality upon less laziness and resignation than this temporary sojourner in Massachusetts. It is a common notion that the world (meaning the people in it) has become tame and commonplace, lost its primeval freshness and epigrammatic point. Mandeville, in his argumentative way, dissents from this entirely. He says that the world is more complex, varied, and a thousand times as interesting as it was in what we call its youth, and that it is as fresh, as individual and capable of producing odd and eccentric characters as ever. He thought the creative vim had not in any degree abated, that both the types of men and of nations are as sharply stamped and defined as ever they were.

Backlog Studies

Was there ever, he said, in the past, any figure more clearly cut and freshly minted than the Yankee? Had the Old World anything to show more positive and uncompromising in all the elements of character than the Englishman? And if the edges of these were being rounded off, was there not developing in the extreme West a type of men different from all preceding, which the world could not yet define? He believed that the production of original types was simply infinite.

Herbert urged that he must at least admit that there was a freshness of legend and poetry in what we call the primeval peoples that is wanting now; the mythic period is gone, at any rate.

Mandeville could not say about the myths. We couldn't tell what interpretation succeeding ages would put upon our lives and history and literature when they have become remote and shadowy. But we need not go to antiquity for epigrammatic wisdom, or for characters as racy of the fresh earth as those handed down to us from the dawn of history. He would put Benjamin Franklin against any of the sages of the mythic or the classic period. He would have been perfectly at home in ancient Athens, as Socrates would have been in modern Boston. There might have been more heroic characters at the siege of Troy than Abraham Lincoln, but there was not one more strongly marked individually; not one his superior in what we call primeval craft and humor. He was just the man, if he could not have dislodged Priam by a writ of ejectment, to have invented the wooden horse, and then to have made Paris the hero of some ridiculous story that would have set all Asia in a roar.

Mandeville said further, that as to poetry, he did not know much about that, and there was not much he cared to read except parts of Shakespeare and Homer, and passages of Milton. But it did seem to him that we had men nowadays, who could, if they would give their minds to it, manufacture in quantity the same sort of epigrammatic sayings and legends that our scholars were digging out of the Orient. He did not know why Emerson in antique setting was not as good as Saadi. Take for instance, said Mandeville, such a legend as this, and how easy it would be to make others like it:

The son of an Emir had red hair, of which he was ashamed, and wished to dye it. But his father said: "Nay, my son, rather behave in such a manner that all fathers shall wish their sons had red hair."

This was too absurd. Mandeville had gone too far, except in the opinion of Our Next Door, who declared that an imitation was just as good as an original, if you could not detect it. But Herbert said that the closer an imitation is to an original, the more unendurable it is. But nobody could tell exactly why.

The Fire–Tender said that we are imposed on by forms. The nuggets of wisdom that are dug out of the Oriental and remote literatures would often prove to be only commonplace if stripped of their quaint setting. If you gave an Oriental twist to some of our modern thought, its value would be greatly enhanced for many people.

I have seen those, said the Mistress, who seem to prefer dried fruit to fresh; but I like the strawberry and the peach of each season, and for me the last is always the best.

Even the Parson admitted that there were no signs of fatigue or decay in the creative energy of the world; and if it is a question of Pagans, he preferred Mandeville to Saadi.

ELEVENTH STUDY

It happened, or rather, to tell the truth, it was contrived,—for I have waited too long for things to turn up to have much faith in "happen," that we who have sat by this hearthstone before should all be together on Christmas eve. There was a splendid backlog of hickory just beginning to burn with a glow that promised to grow more fiery till long past midnight, which would have needed no apology in a loggers' camp,—not so much as the religion of which a lady (in a city which shall be nameless) said, "If you must have a religion, this one will do nicely."

There was not much conversation, as is apt to be the case when people come together who have a great deal to say, and are intimate enough to permit the freedom of silence. It was Mandeville who suggested that we read something, and the Young Lady, who was in a mood to enjoy her own thoughts, said, "Do." And finally it came about that the Fire Tender, without more resistance to the urging than was becoming, went to his library, and returned with a manuscript, from which he read the story of

MY UNCLE IN INDIA

Backlog Studies

Not that it is my uncle, let me explain. It is Polly's uncle, as I very well know, from the many times she has thrown him up to me, and is liable so to do at any moment. Having small expectations myself, and having wedded Polly when they were smaller, I have come to feel the full force, the crushing weight, of her lightest remark about "My Uncle in India." The words as I write them convey no idea of the tone in which they fall upon my ears. I think it is the only fault of that estimable woman, that she has an "uncle in India" and does not let him quietly remain there. I feel quite sure that if I had an uncle in Botany Bay, I should never, never throw him up to Polly in the way mentioned. If there is any jar in our quiet life, he is the cause of it; all along of possible "expectations" on the one side calculated to overawe the other side not having expectations. And yet I know that if her uncle in India were this night to roll a barrel of "India's golden sands," as I feel that he any moment may do, into our sitting–room, at Polly's feet, that charming wife, who is more generous than the month of May, and who has no thought but for my comfort in two worlds, would straightway make it over to me, to have and to hold, if I could lift it, forever and forever. And that makes it more inexplicable that she, being a woman, will continue to mention him in the way she does.

In a large and general way I regard uncles as not out of place in this transitory state of existence. They stand for a great many possible advantages. They are liable to "tip" you at school, they are resources in vacation, they come grandly in play about the holidays, at which season my heart always did warm towards them with lively expectations, which were often turned into golden solidities; and then there is always the prospect, sad to a sensitive mind, that uncles are mortal, and, in their timely taking off, may prove as generous in the will as they were in the deed. And there is always this redeeming possibility in a niggardly uncle. Still there must be something wrong in the character of the uncle per se, or all history would not agree that nepotism is such a dreadful thing.

But, to return from this unnecessary digression, I am reminded that the charioteer of the patient year has brought round the holiday time. It has been a growing year, as most years are. It is very pleasant to see how the shrubs in our little patch of ground widen and thicken and bloom at the right time, and to know that the great trees have added a layer to their trunks. To be sure, our garden,— which I planted under Polly's directions, with seeds that must have been patented, and I forgot to buy the right of, for they are mostly still waiting the final resurrection,—gave evidence that it shared in the misfortune of the Fall, and was never an Eden from which one would have required to have been driven. It was the easiest garden to keep the neighbor's pigs and hens out of I ever saw. If its increase was small its temptations were smaller, and that is no little recommendation in this world of temptations. But, as a general thing, everything has grown, except our house. That little cottage, over which Polly presides with grace enough to adorn a palace, is still small outside and smaller inside; and if it has an air of comfort and of neatness, and its rooms are cozy and sunny by day and cheerful by night, and it is bursting with books, and not unattractive with modest pictures on the walls, which we think do well enough until my uncle—(but never mind my uncle, now),—and if, in the long winter evenings, when the largest lamp is lit, and the chestnuts glow in embers, and the kid turns on the spit, and the house–plants are green and flowering, and the ivy glistens in the firelight, and Polly sits with that contented, far–away look in her eyes that I like to see, her fingers busy upon one of those cruel mysteries which have delighted the sex since Penelope, and I read in one of my fascinating law–books, or perhaps regale ourselves with a taste of Montaigne,—if all this is true, there are times when the cottage seems small; though I can never find that Polly thinks so, except when she sometimes says that she does not know where she should bestow her uncle in it, if he should suddenly come back from India.

There it is, again. I sometimes think that my wife believes her uncle in India to be as large as two ordinary men; and if her ideas of him are any gauge of the reality, there is no place in the town large enough for him except the Town Hall. She probably expects him to come with his bungalow, and his sedan, and his palanquin, and his elephants, and his retinue of servants, and his principalities, and his powers, and his ha—(no, not that), and his chowchow, and his—I scarcely know what besides.

Christmas eve was a shiny cold night, a creaking cold night, a placid, calm, swingeing cold night.

Out–doors had gone into a general state of crystallization. The snow–fields were like the vast Arctic ice–fields that Kane looked on, and lay sparkling under the moonlight, crisp and Christmasy, and all the crystals on the trees and bushes hung glistening, as if ready, at a breath of air, to break out into metallic ringing, like a million silver joy–bells. I mentioned the conceit to Polly, as we stood at the window, and she said it reminded her of Jean Paul. She is a woman of most remarkable discernment.

Christmas is a great festival at our house in a small way. Among the many delightful customs we did not inherit from our Pilgrim Fathers, there is none so pleasant as that of giving presents at this season. It is the most exciting time of the year. No one is too rich to receive something, and no one too poor to give a trifle. And in the act of giving and receiving these tokens of regard, all the world is kin for once, and brighter for this transient glow of generosity. Delightful custom! Hard is the lot of childhood that knows nothing of the visits of Kriss Kringle, or the stockings hung by the chimney at night; and cheerless is any age that is not brightened by some Christmas gift, however humble. What a mystery of preparation there is in the preceding days, what planning and plottings of surprises! Polly and I keep up the custom in our simple way, and great is the perplexity to express the greatest amount of affection with a limited outlay. For the excellence of a gift lies in its appropriateness rather than in its value. As we stood by the window that night, we wondered what we should receive this year, and indulged in I know not what little hypocrisies and deceptions.

I wish, said Polly, "that my uncle in India would send me a camel's–hair shawl, or a string of pearls, each as big as the end of my thumb."

"Or a white cow, which would give golden milk, that would make butter worth seventy–five cents a pound," I added, as we drew the curtains, and turned to our chairs before the open fire.

It is our custom on every Christmas eve—as I believe I have somewhere said, or if I have not, I say it again, as the member from Erin might remark—to read one of Dickens's Christmas stories. And this night, after punching the fire until it sent showers of sparks up the chimney, I read the opening chapter of "Mrs. Lirriper's Lodgings," in my best manner, and handed the book to Polly to continue; for I do not so much relish reading aloud the succeeding stories of Mr. Dickens's annual budget, since he wrote them, as men go to war in these days, by substitute. And Polly read on, in her melodious voice, which is almost as pleasant to me as the Wasser– fluth of Schubert, which she often plays at twilight; and I looked into the fire, unconsciously constructing stories of my own out of the embers. And her voice still went on, in a sort of running accompaniment to my airy or fiery fancies.

"Sleep?" said Polly, stopping, with what seemed to me a sort of crash, in which all the castles tumbled into ashes.

Backlog Studies

"Not in the least," I answered brightly never heard anything more agreeable." And the reading flowed on and on and on, and I looked steadily into the fire, the fire, fire, fi....

Suddenly the door opened, and into our cozy parlor walked the most venerable personage I ever laid eyes on, who saluted me with great dignity. Summer seemed to have burst into the room, and I was conscious of a puff of Oriental airs, and a delightful, languid tranquillity. I was not surprised that the figure before me was clad in full turban, baggy drawers, and a long loose robe, girt about the middle with a rich shawl. Followed him a swart attendant, who hastened to spread a rug upon which my visitor sat down, with great gravity, as I am informed they do in farthest Ind. The slave then filled the bowl of a long-stemmed chibouk, and, handing it to his master, retired behind him and began to fan him with the most prodigious palm-leaf I ever saw. Soon the fumes of the delicate tobacco of Persia pervaded the room, like some costly aroma which you cannot buy, now the entertainment of the Arabian Nights is discontinued.

Looking through the window I saw, if I saw anything, a palanquin at our door, and attendant on it four dusky, half-naked bearers, who did not seem to fancy the splendor of the night, for they jumped about on the snow crust, and I could see them shiver and shake in the keen air. Oho! thought!, this, then, is my uncle from India!

"Yes, it is," now spoke my visitor extraordinary, in a gruff, harsh voice.

"I think I have heard Polly speak of you," I rejoined, in an attempt to be civil, for I did n't like his face any better than I did his voice,—a red, fiery, irascible kind of face.

"Yes I've come over to O Lord,—quick, Jamsetzee, lift up that foot,--take care. There, Mr. Trimings, if that's your name, get me a glass of brandy, stiff."

I got him our little apothecary-labeled bottle and poured out enough to preserve a whole can of peaches. My uncle took it down without a wink, as if it had been water, and seemed relieved. It was a very pleasant uncle to have at our fireside on Christmas eve, I felt.

At a motion from my uncle, Jamsetzee handed me a parcel which I saw was directed to Polly, which I untied, and lo! the most wonderful camel's-hair shawl that ever was, so fine that I immediately drew it through my finger-ring, and so large that I saw it would entirely cover our little room if I spread it out; a dingy red color, but splendid in appearance from the little white hieroglyphic worked in one corner, which is always worn outside, to show that it cost nobody knows how many thousands of dollars.

"A Christmas trifle for Polly. I have come home—as I was saying when that confounded twinge took me—to settle down; and I intend to make Polly my heir, and live at my ease and enjoy life. Move that leg a little, Jamsetzee."

I meekly replied that I had no doubt Polly would be delighted to see her dear uncle, and as for inheriting, if it came to that, I did n't know any one with a greater capacity for that than she.

"That depends," said the gruff old smoker, "how I like ye. A fortune, scraped up in forty years in Ingy, ain't to be thrown away in a minute. But what a house this is to live in!"; the uncomfortable old relative went on, throwing a contemptuous glance round the humble cottage. "Is this all of it?"

"In the winter it is all of it," I said, flushing up; but in the summer, when the doors and windows are open, it is as large as anybody's house. And," I went on, with some warmth, "it was large enough just before you came in, and pleasant enough. And besides, I said, rising into indignation, "you can not get anything much better in this city short of eight hundred dollars a year, payable first days of January, April, July, and October, in advance, and my salary...."

"Hang your salary, and confound your impudence and your seven–by–nine hovel! Do you think you have anything to say about the use of my money, scraped up in forty years in Ingy? THINGS HAVE GOT TO BE CHANGED!" he burst out, in a voice that rattled the glasses on the sideboard.

I should think they were. Even as I looked into the little fireplace it enlarged, and there was an enormous grate, level with the floor, glowing with seacoal; and a magnificent mantel carved in oak, old and brown; and over it hung a landscape, wide, deep, summer in the foreground with all the gorgeous coloring of the tropics, and beyond hills of blue and far mountains lying in rosy light. I held my breath as I looked down the marvelous perspective. Looking round for a second, I caught a glimpse of a Hindoo at each window, who vanished as if they had been whisked off by enchantment; and the close walls that shut us in fled away. Had cohesion and gravitation given out? Was it the "Great Consummation" of the year 18–? It was all like the swift transformation of a dream, and I pinched my arm to make sure that I was not the subject of some diablerie.

The little house was gone; but that I scarcely minded, for I had suddenly come into possession of my wife's castle in Spain. I sat in a spacious, lofty apartment, furnished with a princely magnificence. Rare pictures adorned the walls, statues looked down from deep niches, and over both the dark ivy of England ran and drooped in graceful luxuriance. Upon the heavy tables were costly, illuminated volumes; luxurious chairs and ottomans invited to easy rest; and upon the ceiling Aurora led forth all the flower–strewing daughters of the dawn in brilliant frescoes. Through the open doors my eyes wandered into magnificent apartment after apartment. There to the south, through folding–doors, was the splendid library, with groined roof, colored light streaming in through painted windows, high shelves stowed with books, old armor hanging on the walls, great carved oaken chairs about a solid oaken table, and beyond a conservatory of flowers and plants with a fountain springing in the center, the splashing of whose waters I could hear. Through the open windows I looked upon a lawn, green with close–shaven turf, set with ancient trees, and variegated with parterres of summer plants in bloom. It was the month of June, and the smell of roses was in the air.

I might have thought it only a freak of my fancy, but there by the fireplace sat a stout, red–faced, puffy–looking man, in the ordinary dress of an English gentleman, whom I had no difficulty in recognizing as my uncle from India.

"One wants a fire every day in the year in this confounded climate," remarked that amiable old person, addressing no one in particular.

I had it on my lips to suggest that I trusted the day would come when he would have heat enough to satisfy him, in permanent supply. I wish now that I had.

I think things had changed. For now into this apartment, full of the morning sunshine, came sweeping with the air of a countess born, and a maid of honor bred, and a queen in expectancy, my Polly, stepping with that lofty grace which I always knew she possessed, but which she never had space to exhibit in our little cottage, dressed with that elegance and richness that I should not have deemed possible to the most Dutch duchess that ever lived, and, giving me a complacent nod of recognition, approached her uncle, and said in her smiling, cheery way, "How is the dear uncle this morning?" And, as she spoke, she actually bent down and kissed his horrid old cheek, red–hot with currie and brandy and all the biting pickles I can neither eat nor name, kissed him, and I did not turn into stone.

"Comfortable as the weather will permit, my darling!"—and again I did not turn into stone.

"Wouldn't uncle like to take a drive this charming morning?" Polly asked.

Uncle finally grunted out his willingness, and Polly swept away again to prepare for the drive, taking no more notice of me than if I had been a poor assistant office lawyer on a salary. And soon the carriage was at the door, and my uncle, bundled up like a mummy, and the charming Polly drove gayly away.

How pleasant it is to be married rich, I thought, as I arose and strolled into the library, where everything was elegant and prim and neat, with no scraps of paper and piles of newspapers or evidences of literary slovenness on the table, and no books in attractive disorder, and where I seemed to see the legend staring at me from all the walls, "No smoking." So I uneasily lounged out of the house. And a magnificent house it was, a palace, rather, that seemed to frown upon and bully insignificant me with its splendor, as I walked away from it towards town.

And why town? There was no use of doing anything at the dingy office. Eight hundred dollars a year! It wouldn't keep Polly in gloves, let alone dressing her for one of those fashionable entertainments to which we went night after night. And so, after a weary day with nothing in it, I went home to dinner, to find my uncle quite chirruped up with his drive, and Polly regnant, sublimely engrossed in her new world of splendor, a dazzling object of admiration to me, but attentive and even tender to that hypochondriacal, gouty old subject from India.

Yes, a magnificent dinner, with no end of servants, who seemed to know that I couldn't have paid the wages of one of them, and plate and courses endless. I say, a miserable dinner, on the edge of which seemed to sit by permission of somebody, like an invited poor relation, who wishes he had sent a regret, and longing for some of those nice little dishes that Polly used to set before me with beaming face, in the dear old days.

And after dinner, and proper attention to the comfort for the night of our benefactor, there was the Blibgims's party. No long, confidential interviews, as heretofore, as to what she should wear and what I should wear, and whether it would do to wear it again. And Polly went in one coach, and I in another. No crowding into the hired hack, with all the delightful care about tumbling dresses, and getting there in good order; and no coming home together to our little cozy cottage, in a pleasant, excited state of "flutteration," and sitting down to talk it all over, and "Was n't it nice?" and "Did I look as well as anybody?" and "Of course you did to me," and all that nonsense. We lived in a grand way now, and had our separate establishments and separate plans, and I used to think that a real separation couldn't make matters much different. Not that Polly meant to be any different, or was, at heart; but, you know, she was so much absorbed in her new life of splendor, and perhaps I was a little old–fashioned.

I don't wonder at it now, as I look back. There was an army of dressmakers to see, and a world of shopping to do, and a houseful of servants to manage, and all the afternoon for calls, and her dear, dear friend, with the artless manners and merry heart of a girl, and the dignity and grace of a noble woman, the dear friend who lived in the house of the Seven Gables, to consult about all manner of im– portant things. I could not, upon my honor, see that there was any place for me, and I went my own way, not that there was much comfort in it.

And then I would rather have had charge of a hospital ward than take care of that uncle. Such coddling as he needed, such humoring of whims. And I am bound to say that Polly could n't have been more dutiful to him if he had been a Hindoo idol. She read to him and talked to him, and sat by him with her embroidery, and was patient with his crossness, and wearied herself, that I could see, with her devoted ministrations.

I fancied sometimes she was tired of it, and longed for the old homely simplicity. I was. Nepotism had no charms for me. There was nothing that I could get Polly that she had not. I could surprise her with no little delicacies or trifles, delightedly bought with money saved for the purpose. There was no more coming home weary with office work and being met at the door with that warm, loving welcome which the King of England could not buy. There was no long evening when we read alternately from some favorite book, or laid our deep housekeeping plans, rejoiced in a good bargain or made light of a poor one, and were contented and merry with little. I recalled with longing my little den, where in the midst of the literary disorder I love, I wrote those stories for the "Antarctic" which

Backlog Studies

Polly, if nobody else, liked to read. There was no comfort for me in my magnificent library. We were all rich and in splendor, and our uncle had come from India. I wished, saving his soul, that the ship that brought him over had foundered off Barnegat Light. It would always have been a tender and regretful memory to both of us. And how sacred is the memory of such a loss!

Christmas? What delight could I have in long solicitude and ingenious devices touching a gift for Polly within my means, and hitting the border line between her necessities and her extravagant fancy? A drove of white elephants would n't have been good enough for her now, if each one carried a castle on his back.

"—and so they were married, and in their snug cottage lived happy ever after."—It was Polly's voice, as she closed the book.

"There, I don't believe you have heard a word of it," she said half complainingly.

"Oh, yes, I have," I cried, starting up and giving the fire a jab with the poker; "I heard every word of it, except a few at the close I was thinking"—I stopped, and looked round.

"Why, Polly, where is the camel's-hair shawl?"

"Camel's-hair fiddlestick! Now I know you have been asleep for an hour."

And, sure enough, there was n't any camel's-hair shawl there, nor any uncle, nor were there any Hindoos at our windows.

And then I told Polly all about it; how her uncle came back, and we were rich and lived in a palace and had no end of money, but she didn't seem to have time to love me in it all, and all the comfort of the little house was blown away as by the winter wind. And Polly vowed, half in tears, that she hoped her uncle never would come back, and she wanted nothing that we had not, and she wouldn't exchange our independent comfort and snug house, no, not for anybody's mansion. And then and there we made it all up, in a manner too particular for me to mention; and I never, to this day, heard Polly allude to My Uncle in India.

And then, as the clock struck eleven, we each produced from the place where we had hidden them the modest Christmas gifts we had prepared for each other, and what surprise there was! "Just the thing I needed." And, "It's perfectly lovely." And, "You should n't have done it." And, then, a question I never will answer, "Ten? fifteen? five? twelve?" "My dear, it cost eight hundred dollars, for I have put my whole year into it, and I wish it was a thousand times better."

And so, when the great iron tongue of the city bell swept over the snow the twelve strokes that announced Christmas day, if there was anywhere a happier home than ours, I am glad of it!

Printed in the United States
19734LVS00002B/229